THE CRACK

ff

EMMA TENNANT

The Crack

faber and faber

LONDON · BOSTON

First published in 1973
as *The Time of the Crack*
by Jonathan Cape Limited
First published in this edition in 1985
by Faber and Faber Limited
3 Queen Square London WC1N 3AU

Printed in Great Britain by
Whitstable Litho Limited
Whitstable Kent
All rights reserved

British Library Cataloguing in Publication Data

Tennant, Emma
[The time of the crack] The crack
I. Title   II. The crack
832'.914[F]   PR6070.E52
ISBN 0-571-13482-3

CONTENTS

1

Love at the Playboy

A big funfair was in full swing in Hyde Park. Volleys of shots from the rifle range echoed down Park Lane and the screams from the Big Dipper made the patients in St George's Hospital restless.

Simon Mangrove rose from his sunken bath in the penthouse suite of the Hilton Hotel and strode over to the window to look out. A huge Catherine Wheel, each spoke carrying its little boxload of passengers, threw orange and green reflections against the plate glass—and for a moment his face, the image already distorted by the curve of the window, looked back at him with the crude colours of a medieval devil. Somewhere far below the dodgems crashed and reversed with a grating, metallic sound.

Simon Mangrove's watch announced that it was seven thirty. He pulled off his bathrobe and changed with care into a vicuna suit and a Turnbull & Asser shirt made up for him from specially woven Moroccan cotton. He had decided this evening, his last night before flying back to the States, to visit the Playboy and make a night of it. His wife Rene—the third—would be waiting in New York full of reproaches and he might as well enjoy himself while he could. Why didn't you call me?

Where were you last weekend? He could hear her voice, once so soft and tentative, assume its nagging, whining note. Idly, as he combed his glossy hair and stood back in front of the mirror, Simon Mangrove decided on another divorce.

Park Lane was full of curious people who were examining the funfair from outside and hadn't quite made up their minds to go in yet. Mangrove glanced at the crowd with an amused air: it seemed strange that grown men and women should obtain pleasure from such childish pursuits. Still, it was the Las Vegas of the poor, he supposed. The very thought of spinning through the air in a smelly little wagon made him feel sick. And the smell of the crowd! They were behaving just like a bunch of children, too, those who were inside the funfair, waving the bright sweet candyfloss like emblems of permanent immaturity. Mangrove quickened his step and arrived under the illuminated bunny of the Playboy Club.

As he reached the step, a deafening sound—it was like the outsize rattles of a legion of giant babies—broke out in the street behind him. There was laughter from the crowd, and a derisive cheer. Four big black cars had drawn up outside the entrance to the funfair and men, bearded and in black gowns, were stepping from the cars and waving the rattles as they went in. Mangrove wondered if they were Arabs. Was this a Trade Fair of some description? He glanced up at the banner over the admission gate and then smiled to himself again.

INTERNATIONAL CONVENTION OF
PSYCHOANALYSIS

The lettering was amateurishly done, as if a child had

daubed on the paint. One of the gowned men turned and gave a mock salute to the crowd. More laughter. One of my countrymen, Mangrove thought bitterly. An American. And now the English were getting just as bad.

The weird, caftaned shapes disappeared into the funfair and Mangrove slid through the portals of the Playboy, relieved to see the friendly receptionist and his own image on the closed-circuit TV screen. Here all was as he wanted it—a couple of dry martinis smooth as polished glass, a tasselled menu which offered tonight a swordfish steak with Samoa sauce. He ordered it, leaning back on the banquette to enjoy the tinkling music from the piano.

And here was Baba. Her tail waggled as she brought him his second drink and slid on to the banquette beside him. Baba's father was a clergyman—or so she said—and Mangrove liked to imagine an austere English vicarage with an exotic flower like Baba growing amongst the dull weeds of matins and vespers and collections for the poor. He gave her an affectionate pat and sipped at his drink.

'Baba, will you marry me?' He was almost surprised himself to hear the words come out. But, after all, why not? Baba was friendly and gentle, and obviously very much impressed by Mangrove.

'Marry you?' Baba giggled. 'I thought you were married already, Simon.'

Mangrove burst out laughing. 'What age are you living in, sweetie?' Then he assumed a more serious expression. 'That's what I like about the English, Baba. So old-fashioned. No'—as Baba pouted—'I really mean this. Rene—that's my wife—and me, we haven't been getting along for months now. I shan't even see her when I arrive in New York. Promise!'

He really did mean it too, he thought with a surge of confidence. A new life with Baba—that was the thing.

'Would we live in America?' Baba asked.

But at that point the piano stopped playing and a soft pink light diffused the bar. As the floorshow started up, a waiter arrived with Mangrove's swordfish steak, and Baba, with a little hushed scream, wriggled out of the banquette.

'I'm in the show tonight,' she gasped. 'And I'm late.'

Her breasts hung for a moment over Mangrove's plate as she stooped to kiss him. The waiter deposited a little dollop of Samoa sauce by the side of the inanimate swordfish.

'I'll be waiting,' Mangrove promised. 'Shake it for me and me only, Baba.'

Baba Goes for a Ride

Joseph Thirsk, analyst-in-chief of the Regress Centre, boarded the Big Dipper with his crew of a hundred patients. They were all in a state of high excitement, shouting and gripping the sides of the little wagons and screaming in high-pitched voices as the climb to the dizzy summit began. Some of them had regressed beyond childhood and had arrived at the womb; and these Joseph Thirsk kept near him. They sat in coiled, foetal positions and looked out uncomprehendingly at the bright lights of the funfair. Thirsk hoped the shock of the Big Dipper would jolt them into the birth trauma, and watched them carefully in the few sickening moments of suspense before the great swooping fall down the track.

In a booth which bore the legend MEDEA, CLAIR-VOYANT AND PALMIST: THE VOICE FROM THE ANCIENT WORLD, a veiled woman shuffled a deck of cards and dusted down the crystal globe. She had a good reputation, and a small queue waited outside for a consultation. But this evening several customers had left irritated and disappointed. Medea had only one message to give to women and men alike. And it wasn't enough.

'What does it mean, I'm going to cross the water?'

one woman asked crossly as she pushed her way out of the booth. 'That's what they used to say a hundred years ago. And she wouldn't tell me anything else either.'

'Ask for your money back,' suggested one of the strolling analysts, who was examining the reactions of the people to the various sideshows. 'You shouldn't let yourself get taken for a ride like that.'

'I think I will.' The woman glanced at him gratefully. 'I mean, I could set up myself and tell people that and make a packet out of it. Couldn't I?'

'You certainly could,' the analyst reassured her, scribbling in his notebook. He wrote: 'Anal Retentive, Manic symptoms,' and popped it back in his pocket. 'Go in there now and confront her with her dishonesty,' he went on with an encouraging smile.

The woman elbowed her way through the queue and pushed into the booth. 'I've got something to tell you—' she began. Then stopped. Medea, no longer veiled, faced her across the narrow counter.

Terrified, the woman shrank back against the faded red plush curtains. Only a whimper escaped from her mouth as Medea spoke.

'Go. There is little time left to you. Cross the water.'

Medea's eyes were black and her hair so white that the darkness of the booth was illumined on all sides, making a bright circle round the crouching woman.

'The water is sinking ... The bridge is stretched to exhaustion ... the dead earth drinks its last.'

With these words, Medea turned and vanished through the curtain at the back. In the vacuum of her non-existence the booth was plunged into sudden night.

The woman screamed and staggered out into the

myriad brightly coloured lights of the funfair. She collapsed at the feet of the analyst.

He picked her up, pausing first to jot the stage of her regression in his notebook. 'Rapid descent to Oral,' he wrote. 'Occasioned by prediction.' Then, helping to support her with his arm, he led her towards the Big Dipper. A large crowd of people, rounded up by the other strolling analysts, waited there for their turn.

By midnight the shrieks from the funfair were so loud that the visitors to the Playboy Club wandered out on to the steps and stood with amused expressions as they watched the childlike cavorting in the park. Amongst them were Mangrove and Baba, who had just celebrated their engagement with a bottle of champagne.

'Darling!' Baba tugged at Mangrove's arm. 'Let's go in for a moment, shall we? Just for a little whirl?'

'O.K.'

Baba sounded wifely and possessive already, Mangrove thought with gloom. And the last thing he felt like doing after sipping champagne in the Playboy was being thrown up in the air like a sack of potatoes. He nodded agreement, however, and they crossed into the park.

Several of the analysts looked curiously at Baba—she still had her ears and tail, had slipped on a wrap over her costume—but it was Mangrove who was stopped by one of the tall black-gowned brotherhood and questioned.

'I don't see why you want to talk to me,' Mangrove said nervously. 'I'm just a normal kind of person. What's the idea with all this funfair business anyway?'

'We're studying regression.' The bearded man gave an earnest nod of the head. 'Up there for instance, in the Big Dipper, multiple births are taking place. You could almost call that extraordinary machine a giant Fertility Drug. Feel like going on it yourself?'

'No thanks.' Mangrove tried to edge away without the analyst noticing.

'The rifle range perhaps?'

'No—no.'

'Bumper cars?'

'Bumper cars,' Mangrove repeated with a laugh. 'I think I might have grown out of them, you know.'

'Oh do let's go on the bumper cars,' Baba cried. 'I used to *love* them when I was a kid. Simon?'

This was really too much, Simon thought. It turned out he'd become engaged to a child of five, not a grown woman. And the analyst was looking at her with keen interest now, seeing for the first time the tail that bulged under her coat and the waggling ears on her head.

'Very well, very well.'

More to escape the man than to gratify Baba's whim, Simon took her arm and led her towards the bumper cars. They climbed into a miniature Bugatti, Baba squealing with delight.

No sooner was Simon behind the wheel than the old excitement of racing came back to him and he was bearing down aggressively on the other cars, spinning the wheel as he rammed the bonnet into the already dented metal. Baba's ears flopped wildly from side to side as he accelerated at top speed into the centre of the course.

'Oh, Simon!' she gasped, 'watch out!'

Coming towards them at full speed was a violent-looking boy of about fifteen in the only other sports car— a yellow Porsche. In spite of the tiny dimensions of both cars, and the fact that the drivers' knees were practically under their chins, there was a genuine thrill in the confrontation and Simon found himself gritting his teeth and swearing under his breath. Ten feet ... five feet ...

'Stop!' Baba screamed.

Crash! The cars met head on. The deafening sound of the colliding cars set up a chorus of oohs and aahs from the people round the track. Then someone shrieked with real fear. Flames were springing up from the twisted bonnets and an acrid smell filled the air.

'Can't reverse!' Simon yelled at the boy. 'We're stuck!'

Uselessly, he stabbed at the accelerator. The orange flames leapt high. An attendant ran forward, and strong arms pulled Baba out of the car. The flames licked contentedly at the boy in the yellow Porsche and then turned to run with sly speed in the direction of the Bugatti passenger seat.

Both Simon and the occupant of the Porsche were jammed in their seats, the toy dashboards across their chests like steel bars. Silent now, the crowd formed a semicircle at a distance of ten feet from the conflagration.

Then all the lights went out. At first, there was no reaction from the crowd; like moths they were held entranced by the merry fire, the movement of the orange spikes as they shot roof-high. Then everyone realized at once what had happened. The whole funfair had fused. A gelatinous darkness made itself felt in every chest, a suffocating black blanket came down like a hangman's noose. From the stranded patients in the Big Dipper the first screams of terror came through the windless air.

'It's everywhere!' The attendant holding Baba relaxed his grip as he scanned Park Lane and the Hilton and the distant swirl of Hyde Park Corner. The bright lights of the

fair had gone out. Only the flames from the charred cars
continued to eat their way busily through vicuna suit and
Levis, bumpers and imitation racing tyres.

'My god!' Baba hardly recognized her own voice, a
low croaking sound. Released by the attendant, she found
herself wandering, dazed, away from the flames and
down a step on to the ground. Above her towered the
Big Wheel, motionless, the passengers in the invisible
boxes calling out for help and shouting conflicting sug-
gestions. She stumbled on, her mind numb. Soon the
light from the flames died down. People were bumped
against—some of them as soft as bales of cloth and others
sharp and angular. Objects—flags probably or the coats of
people who were trying to let themselves down from
stranded wagons—brushed across her face. The funfair
had become a gigantic ghost train.

And there was no moon! Even in her semi-conscious
state, Baba realized that this total darkness was something
she had never known before in her life. A sort of vertigo
overtook her, and she put her hands out in front of her for
support. Perhaps Simon would be there—perhaps it was
all a bad dream and she would wake in his suite in the
Hilton. Like last night. Only this was tonight. All the
same, power cuts in London were common enough. How
Simon would laugh at the British strikes—how he
would—

But every moment it became clearer to Baba that
Simon was dead. She stopped, looking down at where her
feet presumably were. If only she could see her feet! It
was such a simple thing to ask. And she never wanted
anything more.

She looked up again. A tiny flicker of hope flitted

16

across her mind. Something white—strangely phos-phorescent, like the light from a crowd of fireflies—was moving just ahead of her. She followed it, stretching out her hand. Her fingers met a substance that yielded and flew apart under her touch, then closed again round her hand and bathed her wrist with the same pale radiance.

It was hair. Medea Smith turned her head at Baba's touch. Her face, cavernous under the white curtain which fell to her shoulders, had three circles of black in the place of eyes and mouth. Then she turned again and the phantom head moved on through the unseen crowd.

Baba followed.

3

Joining the Ladies

At Sir Max Bowlby's house the ladies left the dining-room
at the end of dinner and the gentlemen were left to their
port and cigars.

Bowlby, a property millionaire, had recently bought
the house in Cheyne Walk and decorated it in the eastern
style, with rich hangings from India and low tables
inlaid with mother-of-pearl. Only his dining-room was
conventional: a long mahogany table, Old Masters on the
walls, and a Waterford glass chandelier which gave out a
million iridescent rays from candles regularly trimmed by
footmen.

Because the dining-room was lit only by candles, Sir
Max Bowlby and his friends were unaware that the lights
had gone out all over London. They were discussing their
property abroad, and Sir Evelyn Jacobs was boasting
that his private island in the Caribbean was worth at least
ten times more than he had paid for it.

'You still can't beat the Med,' Sir Max said comfortably.
'I really cleaned up in Sardinia. And it's a lovely development, mind you.' He always felt constrained to remind
people that there is beauty in money too.

'What I say is', put in Mr Joshua McDougall, 'that this
holiday boom is all very well, but what happens when

there's a depression? People don't take holidays. And what are people always looking for? Flats. Somewhere to live. And where?'

'London,' Sir Max said. 'I agree, Joshua. But—'

'London Development Company will never fail,' McDougall announced with solemnity. 'The entire south-east of England has become the greatest boom area in the history of property speculation.'

At that moment, to Sir Evelyn's slight alarm, the floor seemed to move under his chair. It was as if, the thought flashed through his mind, a large whale had surfaced somewhere under the floorboards and was now edging its way up through the carpet. Sir Evelyn looked accusingly at Sir Max's brandy.

But Sir Max had felt it as well; and the rather weedy little husband of an heiress cousin of Sir Max's gave a squeak of surprise and fear.

'Don't tell me Cheyne Walk is flooding,' Sir Max said sonorously, as if it would immediately stop flooding if he asked it to. 'Did you feel anything, Evelyn?'

Sir Evelyn said he had. With expressions of protective concern, the gentlemen rose to go and find the ladies. Too bad if they were frightened in any way. Sir Max threw open the door, and then stopped.

'That's funny.' He frowned into the black passage. 'All the lights seem to have gone out. Didn't realize there was a power cut this evening.'

'There isn't,' said the weedy husband.

'Your house doesn't seem to be in very good shape,' laughed McDougall.

Lighting a match and paying no attention to this remark, Sir Max went bravely out into the passage. At that moment the floor gave a distinctive heave and the mahogany table subsided slowly on to it like a sheep lying down to die. Porcelain plates and cut-glass goblets rolled on to the carpet and lay still.

'Good God,' said McDougall. 'Did you have the house surveyed properly, Max?'

Bowlby, flickering match in hand, went grimly towards the staircase. The banister jumped nervously back at his touch. As his foot went out to the first step, the entire staircase, with the slow grace of a Chinese paper decoration opening out, arched its back and became an interesting but useless accordion. Bowlby staggered back, to be caught by Sir Evelyn.

'This is preposterous,' McDougall said. 'In property and you can't keep your own house in order. What about my wife? She's up there—probably frightened to death. Where's the phone? We must rescue her at all costs.'

It was well known that McDougall had married a famous model only a few weeks before. None of the other men expressed any concern for their wives, and it was McDougall, gold lighter in hand, who had to grope his way to the phone at the far end of the hall. Hummocks had risen in the passage and he scrambled from one to the other, not noticing that the walls, although still perfectly in line, were contracting quite fast and threatened to squeeze him to death before he attained his goal.

'The phone's dead,' he shouted desperately from his impending grave. 'What's going on here for Christ's sake, Bowlby?'

Upstairs, as the walls of the downstairs hall embraced

Joshua McDougall like the friendly white arms of a male nurse, the women were staring with fascinated horror out of the window. Caught in the middle of powdering their noses by the blackout, they were more friendly towards each other than they would normally have been. Lady Bowlby had been rescued from the bathroom by the new Mrs McDougall, and the traces of animosity which had shown at dinner had now disappeared.

'I just can't believe it,' the heiress married to the weedy husband said. 'I'm so frightened—I—'

'Let's look at it rationally,' suggested Lady Bowlby. 'We can't go down the stairs because they've collapsed. We—'

'How can you be rational about something like this?' said the new Mrs McDougall with a shudder. 'I mean, just look at it now.'

There was silence as they gathered round the window again. Only an occasional sob from the heiress could be heard in the room.

Outside there was the river. But it was a river surprisingly wide. In the light from the few stars great stretches of mud could be seen; broken bridges lay like snapped elastic on the swampy ooze. And—it was difficult to make out—it seemed the Embankment had cracked and fallen down on to the mud below. It was hard to tell if there was any water in the river at all.

'Suppose,' said Mrs McDougall. 'I mean, suppose it's a crack. In the earth's surface. Suppose ... '

'We must wait for the police,' said Lady Bowlby calmly. 'Things are bound to be all right further inland.'

With these comforting words, she stared out of the window again. With another heave, like a man trying to shrug off an overcoat, the house moved several more feet towards the bank of the exhausted river.

4

Women and Children First

In the light of the dying flames from the burning bumper cars, someone had been clever enough to knot together various lengths of rope so that Thirsk's patients could be lowered from the highest cars of the Big Dipper. Subdued, they trotted obediently after him through the darkened funfair.

'I don't know what we're going to do,' Thirsk confided to a lay analyst who was accompanying him, anxious for instructions. 'We can't go North, that's for certain.'

The lay analyst—Harcourt was his name—nodded agreement. Behind them towered the new mountain of North London, the foothills extending as far as Marble Arch. In the grey starlight which had succeeded the total blackness of the cataclysm, it was just possible to make out the jagged peaks and narrow ravines of what once had been Hampstead and Primrose Hill.

'Harley Street will be buried as it deserved to be,' Thirsk said with satisfaction. 'This is an earthquake, I suppose. But in London!'

'Certainly a disaster area,' said Harcourt, who was not famed for his quickness of mind. 'But when's the relief coming? And what is the Government doing about all this, I'd like to know?'

'We'll make for Westminster,' Thirsk said firmly. He had already forgotten his virulent attack of the day before on the British parliamentary system, and his oath to construct an Alternative Society through regression methods.

'A demonstration,' Harcourt agreed warmly. 'This neglect is monstrous!'

'We'll be getting help from the States by morning,' Thirsk reminded him.

'They've cut down on Foreign Aid,' Harcourt put in. 'Suppose we get nothing?'

With this thought in mind, the two doctors walked slowly towards Hyde Park Corner, each stooped over a push-chair. Behind, the older 'children' squabbled and stumbled, some of them sitting down on the churned-up road to remove their shoes and others crying loudly as they were bumped against in the dark. Of Thirsk and Harcourt's two 'babies', Thirsk's was giving the most trouble. A man of thirty-five, Jo-Jo by name, he had only half an hour before been born on the Dipper, and his thin screams echoed through the cold night air. On top of that, his dummy kept slipping from his mouth on to the ruined tarmac and Thirsk had to bend for it, cursing every time as it disappeared under the folds of his black robe. Harcourt's baby, a middle-aged woman with an evil expression and a spiteful way of rocking in the push-chair so that it nearly tilted over at every step, had taken an instant dislike to Jo-Jo—her hands came out like claws whenever she was in reach of him and she had already managed several times to poke him in the eye.

'Well,' Thirsk said gloomily. 'Here we are. What shall we do with them?'

Here was Hyde Park Corner. The fact that it had taken so long to guide the patients along Park Lane clearly showed that their chances of reaching Westminster by morning were low. Thirsk and Harcourt looked at each other, and gravely inclined their heads.

'Yes,' Harcourt said after a while. 'I think they'll do better here.'

'Some of the buildings remain.' He was accustomed to having to justify his decisions. And with the help of the Government we can collect them in the morning.'

'Exactly,' said Harcourt.

Hyde Park Corner was, of course, unrecognizable. The twisted metal of crashed cars lay scattered at the base of the great earth mound that had gone up like a gigantic molehill. Picking their way carefully through the debris, the doctors led their charges to the roofless hospital that once had been St George's.

'Perfectly all right for a few hours,' Thirsk said briskly. He shepherded his charges into the abandoned casualty ward, stepping with care over the stretchered bodies of recent car-crash victims. 'Pity we've got no toys for them though,' he added looking round. 'The fives and over aren't going to like it much here.'

'We're in the middle of a disaster, man,' Harcourt snapped. 'Good for the creative process anyway, to have a period without toys. I thought we'd been through that.'

A man with a bandaged head stirred and groaned loudly at the disturbance. Thirsk went over and peered down at him.

'Look at this,' he chortled. 'The unsevered umbilical cord and its consequences, eh, Harcourt?'

By the side of the patient lay a white-gowned anaesthetist. His hand still firmly clasped the needle which protruded from the patient's arm. Harcourt's worried expression vanished for a moment.

'The death of non-separation,' he agreed. 'This will serve as a lesson to the children.'

The analysts, tiptoeing like two Father Christmases leaving the nursery, left the hospital and struck off in the direction of Westminster. Although some of the buildings seemed to have lost their roofs, the disaster had been less complete here and Piccadilly, if you didn't count the fallen trees in Green Park and the strange new elongated shape of the Ritz, was much as before.

Thirsk and Harcourt strode along at a good speed. 'We're in luck,' Thirsk remarked, 'if you look at the situation objectively. This is just the kind of traumatic shock this society needs to jolt it out of its complacency.'

'Which stems from repressed violence,' Harcourt put in almost before he had finished. 'From the rebirth we should really have something to build on.'

Piccadilly Circus, which had succumbed to the will of the planners before the catastrophe and was now in the first stages of reconstruction, loomed before them. All of the roads out of it were blocked by accumulated rubble and Thirsk and Harcourt stood for a while, perplexed at which turn to take. Behind them, from a first-floor window in the crushed Ritz, an American woman cried for help.

'The death rattle of capitalism,' Thirsk commented as he pulled up his robes and clambered over the debris. 'We'd better make for St James's, I suppose.'

'If only it would get light,' Harcourt complained. 'My God, Joe, what's that?'

On the far side of the ruined circus, a procession advanced. It was led by what appeared, in the dank brown light of early dawn, to be a phantom — tall, evanescent, weightless. Hair as soft and white as a sheep's fleece flowed out over its shoulders and cast a pale glow on the crowd behind.

'Girls! Women!' Harcourt cried. 'Where are they going? Who are they?'

The procession turned down St James's, moving at a stately speed.

'We'll see,' Thirsk muttered grimly. 'Maybe they know something we don't.'

'Oh, they couldn't,' Harcourt panted as he scrambled after Thirsk and slid down a splintery plank on to the ground. 'What about Westminster, Joe? The Prime Minister? I mean ... '

'We follow,' Thirsk barked. Keeping a discreet distance, the two men followed the ghostly parade. The brown of the sky deepened, and the few stars went out.

In the hospital, the children were thoroughly enjoying themselves. The five-year-olds, led by Neddy and Mary, a brother and sister who were regressing together (and who before their rescue by Thirsk had been respectively at Wormword Scrubs and Holloway) were playing doctors in the emergency wards. Neddy, brandishing his scalpel, was striding impatiently from bed to bed as Mary prepared the patients for their operations. He had decided to amputate the leg of a man with a serious heart condition, who was attached to various complicated-looking machines — and it seemed that someone in the latency period would have to be called in from the casualty ward downstairs to help dismantle them. Meanwhile, to the consternation of the new mothers in the maternity section, Jo-Jo and his evil contemporary Mrs Withers had had themselves carried along and placed in the cribs alongside the beds. Jo-Jo, determined to breast-feed, had already half suffocated two women in his attempt to subjugate them to his needs. Mrs Withers cried with a bitterness that was implacable.

Neddy made his incision and then sawed through the leg carefully. In the casualty ward, Tony, a ten-year-old schizophrenic, to whom Thirsk had related with particular success, suddenly found his regression reversing. With a whoop of joy, he felt the onset of adolescence, the bristling of hairs on his chin, the unhealthy desire to rape a patient on an upper floor. His mind a jumble of poetic images, he ran for the stairs.

As Neddy handed the leg gravely to his sister, the screams of the geriatrics as they fell under Tony's wild embraces rang through the hospital.

Meanwhile, Thirsk and Harcourt were losing heart as they followed the fluorescent banner of Medea Smith's hair in the direction of the river.

'They're probably just a crowd of crazies,' Harcourt hissed. His legs were shorter than Thirsk's, and his robe the same length. 'Why don't we cut across to Westminster, for Christ's sake?'

Thirsk simply shook his leonine head in reply. They had arrived at the Kings Road by now, and his white feet, accustomed only to the cork floors of the Regression Centre, had developed blisters. In spite of his hobbling gait, Harcourt reflected, he looked splendid, almost prophetic. Comparisons with Moses and Karl Marx flashed through the young lay analyst's mind.

Medea and her followers turned down Flood Street. Eyes down, as if staring at the ground would make it go past quicker, the two men went after her. Then Thirsk glanced up, and—a rare occasion for him—gave an involuntary gasp. Harcourt, stumbling over the hem of his robe, bumped into him. They both collapsed on to the pavement at the intersection of Flood Street and Cheyne Walk.

There was no embankment! The broken road, which looked as if a giant tractor, simply for amusement, had ploughed crooked furrows in it and then departed, fell steeply into the mud flats of the drained river-bed. Leaning over it, like slender trees in a high wind, were the houses of Cheyne Walk. Above them towered Rossetti Gardens Mansions, at an angle of forty-five degrees, brooding menacingly over Cheyne Walk like an elephant perched on a ball. Sounds of cracking and straining masonry filled the otherwise unnaturally silent dawn.

Thirsk wiped his spectacles impatiently on his robe. 'I still can't see the other side of the river,' he snorted. 'What about you, Harcourt?'

Medea and her band made their way, without any change of pace, towards the shattered remains of Battersea Bridge. Thirsk and Harcourt, undecided, stood looking after them.

'A split in the river,' Thirsk mused as they picked their way across the road and stared at the almost invisible bank opposite. 'A great crack! D'you see it, Harcourt?'

Harcourt said that he did. Suddenly, after the exhaustion

of the night, he longed to be back in the States. He felt afraid and lonely. He clasped at Thirsk's arm.

'A schizophrenic society indeed,' Thirsk proclaimed.

Harcourt, bursting into tears, whined to be taken home.

5

Hampstead Disturb'd, Little Venice Preserv'd

Jeremy Waters, his second wife, his two stepchildren and three children, the New Zealand au-pair girl and the family pets Adolf the spaniel and Ben the budgie were tipped out of their Hampstead home as the great new hill of North London was formed. They rolled down through the Village and ended up in the foothills, one of which was crowned triumphally by Marble Arch.

Waters—a prominent ecologist and anti-pollutionist—opened his eyes and found himself in what seemed to be a giant rubbish heap. The tiny moment of pleasure that came to him when he recognized the new scrumple-up disposable I.C.I. beercan a few inches from his face was succeeded by terror when he realized that there were several thousand of them—and that they had been thrown up into a towering mountain over a hundred feet high. A thin trickle of lager ran like lava from the summit of the uncertain volcano.

A muffled scream showed the whereabouts of Waters's family. He picked himself up with care and edged round the face of the mountain. Beneath him, as his vision cleared, he was able to see in the brown light, so reminiscent of his worst smog nightmares, a flattish terrain stretching out down Park Lane. What looked like a wrecked funfair stood forlornly amongst the fallen trees in Hyde Park.

Waters's foot stumbled against something hard and metallic.

Although he was not a mystical man, his heart missed a beat. Flying saucer? Spaceship? He tried to remember what his children believed in. What if they had been right all along? He stood staring down at it.

A big red circle. An O. Dropped casually by the new invaders? He looked fearfully up at the sky.

Waters's second stepson leapt towards him over the broken sewage pipes and fragmented pavement.

> Chantilly Lace
> And a pretty face ...
> You KNOW what I like.

Waters's hand swung out and knocked the transistor into silence. 'Rubbishy music to serenade the end of mankind,' he snapped bitterly. For a moment he saw the pop groups of the 'sixties, the art of Andy Warhol and the boutiques of Carnaby Street as directly responsible for the apocalypse—and anger flared up inside him. Then his shoulders sagged and he gave a sigh of resignation. He had known this was going to come. But not so soon.

'I'll change to Radio 3 if you like,' Tommy the stepson offered. He was an obliging boy, and had had to put up with a lot since his mother's remarriage and the move to Hampstead.

'This is no time for Bach or Mozart,' Waters said self-pityingly. 'Where's your mother?'

When Greta, the second wife, and the other children

had been located, Waters suggested in as brisk a tone as possible that they move on to flat ground.

'Regent's Park is our best bet,' he said, as if he had just received a radio message from that quarter. 'Come on, off we go.'

He walked forward purposefully, hoping that no one would notice the ominous red circle behind him. Whatever happened, they must get as far away from it as possible. If it was anything—if it was in fact the transmitting station of the new conquerors of the world—

'Hey, the budgie's dead,' moaned Waters's youngest daughter. 'Poor Ben! Oh, poor Ben.'

Come *on*,' Waters cried in exasperation. 'There may be more dead than the budgerigar, I fear.'

We may be the only survivors, he thought to himself with a pang of fear. And hadn't he longed for the simple life, the camp fire and the homegrown, unsprayed potatoes? How often had he sat in the conservatory in Hampstead dreaming of the day when he and Greta would have a little farm of their own and be entirely self-supporting? After he had done his bit against pollution, of course. But now—if they were the only people left in the world—

'We've got to bury him,' the girl cried. 'Daddy— please!'

With a great effort of willpower, Waters turned back towards the scarlet O. It was in the centre of it, it went without saying, that she was digging a hole for the grave. Children always knew, he thought gloomily.

Then it occurred to him that if they were to be saved from extinction it would be through children.

A strange selection of phrases came into his head.

Suffer little children to come unto me. (Waters had had a very religious upbringing.) The Age of Aquarius. Generation Gap.

That red circle meant something to his daughter.

Visual imagination. Non-verbal communication. Thirsk's theories of regression!

Heart pounding, he watched the little girl lower the corpse of the bird into its last resting-place.

The budgerigar looked exotic now, its plumage bright and mysterious. A sacrifice to the new gods?

He glanced up at the spires of twisted rubble. With a reverence he had never felt even as a child at midnight mass, he gazed at the cathedral of the future. Pillars of broken concrete lamp-posts, flying buttresses made of the half-buried bodies of London buses and cars. Why had he never seen how beautiful it all was?

And sunken too. Multi-level! Multi-media!

Waters turned to his wife with the gleaming eyes of the convert. Motioning her to be quiet, he tiptoed to the scene of the burial. The great red circle lay at his feet like a red-rimmed eye.

When the interment was over, the family walked off in the direction of Regent's Park. Waters felt a strange exaltation at the sight of the cracked streets and collapsed, abandoned houses.

'This is indeed the beginning of a new life,' he confided to Greta.

She nodded wearily.

There were no people anywhere.

The first rays of a cool sun poured through banks of brown cloud as they reached Regent's Park. Waters, in spite of his conversion, gave a tut of dismay. Queen

Mary's rose garden, where he and Greta had so often walked—where he had decided, in fact, to leave his cruel and materialistic first wife—had disappeared under a great mound of dully gleaming metal. Not cars—so what was it? After the first shock, they ran towards it. A needle-thin shaft of sunlight danced over the acres of broken fuselage.

Crashed spacecraft? Waters's hand flew to his face in self-protection. Fall-out? A new interstellar virus escaping invisibly from the tortured cockpit? He walked cautiously towards it.

'A Jumbo,' Waters's third stepson announced in a matter-of-fact voice. 'T.W.A.' Adolf trotted up into the wreck and sniffed about in the remains of the galley, returning with a chunk of tournedos steak in his mouth. A smell of airline food accompanied him.

'I'm hungry!' all the children shouted in unison. 'Can we go up there, Daddy? Can we?'

Before Waters had time to answer, they were scrambling into the stomach of the crashed plane. Adolf snapped ferociously as the first-class passengers' larder was discovered, and its contents taken away from him.

'It's not organic food,' Greta cried. 'Darling, stop them if you can!'

But Waters was puzzling on the same problem that had confronted him all the way from Marble Arch. No people. No passengers on the plane. No one anywhere. He thought once again of the red circle. Had it come to suck all humanity from the planet, and missed out, by some extraordinary chance, the Waters?

'Matter and energy,' he muttered to himself. Then he decided to tell his secret to his wife.

'That big red O.' He paused solemnly. 'You saw it? It is my belief—'

'That was the Odeon Marble Arch under there,' Tommy pointed out. He turned up his transistor and prised open a tin of Persian caviar.

'O for Odeon,' the youngest daughter trilled. 'Ben's buried in a cinema.'

She gave a high laugh and Waters turned away, his heel scraping the edge of the Jumbo's nose. A wave of sadness and despair filled him.

The Nash terraces along Regent's Park had been thrown several hundred feet in the air, so that they resembled a series of slides of the Acropolis in Athens.

With a low murmur of appreciation, Greta got out her camera and started snapping. Waters wandered dejectedly away, skirting the fallen chestnuts in the big avenue.

In the distance, like the sound of tons of water being released from a pent-up dam, something was rushing closer.

At the foot of the splendid pillars of the ruin of Chester Terrace, Waters fell to the ground in fear.

Another crashing Jumbo Jet? A real spacecraft this time? He closed his eyes and waited.

6

Baba Goes to Church

By the time Baba reached the river, her head and her feet were aching so much that she had completely forgotten the strange death of Simon Mangrove. Following Medea seemed the obvious, natural thing to do.

None of the women, who walked, Baba noticed, with an odd determination, as if their destination had been set for them centuries before and they had only just been permitted to reach it, paid any attention to the two robed analysts in their wake. Only one—a girl of about nineteen who told Baba she was called Noreen and worked as a waitress in the Hilton—burst out laughing when Thirsk and Harcourt subsided on to the ground at the corner of Flood Street and what had once been the Embankment.

'No place for them where we're going,' she said with another giggle.

'Why?' Baba asked eagerly. 'Where *are* we going anyway? I don't think I can walk much longer,' she added, close to tears.

'Can't you *feel* where we're going?' Noreen said. She hugged her arms to her body in enthusiasm. 'No more washing up. No more frilly aprons,' she ran on in the quick trilling voice Baba found so attractive. 'Same for you, Baba. No more serving drinks dressed as a rabbit. What do you think?'

Baba reached behind and felt for her furry tail. It was hard to understand Noreen when she talked like this.

'What about the other women?' she said. 'What's in it for them where we're going?'

At this, a head-scarfed woman of about fifty turned round. 'Supper on the table at six when he gets home,' she snapped out. 'Wash it up. Darn the clothes. TV. Bed.'

'No more of that,' suddenly chorused a whole section of the procession.

'Up with the baby at six,' a youngish woman just behind Baba crooned in her ear. 'Cereals for the school-goers. Sausages too. Vacuum the sitting-room.'

'No more of that,' came a strong gust of sturdy voices.

'Stop at the launderette on the way back from work,' the older woman continued. 'Stand in the queue for the food when the shop's closing anyway.'

'No more of that,' Baba muttered with the others. She felt it only polite to join in. But where could this place be that had no cereals or vacuums or TV? She gazed anxiously at Noreen for the answer.

'Now you understand,' Noreen laughed. 'Look, Baba—why don't you do the same?'

There was a chorus of approval as Noreen tugged at her eyelids. A pair of what looked like dead black centipedes fluttered to the ground, and several of the women clapped.

'Do I have to get rid of mine too?' Baba asked miserably. Already she wished that she hadn't chosen to follow Medea to the river. But at the time there had seemed to be no alternative. Cautiously, she glanced either side of her. Whichever way she looked, it was a bad prospect.

The crack in the river-bed had widened even in the short time it took Medea's army to march along Cheyne Walk. It would now be almost impossible to jump across — and other cracks, small still and thin as spiders' webs, were breaking away from it like splintering ice. The opposite bank, only just becoming visible in the thinning brown light, looked ominous and uninviting.

As for the houses in Cheyne Walk, there was little hope of finding asylum there. Leaning drunkenly forward — even moving towards the river, Baba could have sworn — they looked like the exhausted guests at the end of a fancy-dress party. Pale pink façades and climbing clematis gave an air of tired gaiety. In several cases the front door had fallen off its hinges and the black hallways gaped like missing teeth. The only thing to do was to follow Medea.

At the end of Cheyne Walk, Medea turned inland. Silent once more, the women followed her. Baba looked wonderingly about her. No one to be seen. Not a human voice, no sign of life anywhere. She pulled at her bunny ears in perplexity. Were these women the only people left on earth? Had Medea led only women to safety? And if so, why?

It would be sad if all the men had disappeared, Baba thought. Stifling a sigh, she increased her step to match Noreen's and walked the last few steps with as cheerful an air as possible.

For they had reached their destination. Of one accord, the women stopped. Before them — and clearly marked as an early victim of the property men, for a crumpled bulldozer lay beside the building—stood an abandoned church. Children had scrawled obscenities on its walls, and half the roof was missing. But, miraculously, it stood. All round it lay the ruins of Limerston Street and Lamont Road. Only Cheyne Walk, like an upended comb, was visible behind them.

Medea's voice reverberated in the thin, windless air. 'Sisters, this is the Temple. Enter!'

The women went in two by two. Soon the church was filled to overflowing. As they went, although there was no wind outside and nothing stirred, a great rushing sound accompanied them.

7

An Angry Wife Invades the Temple of Women and Sends Baba Flying

It was stiflingly hot in the church, and the chanting voices of Medea and the other women soon sent Baba into a sort of trance. Snatches of the tunes she had danced to in the Playboy mingled with the sonorous wailing:

Our time is come ...
The River is Broken ...
Tell Laura I love her, Our Oppression is Ended ...
Blue suede shoes ...

The murky brown light of the now fully-advanced morning turned the stained glass sombre. Medea's hair was the colour of weed at the bottom of a pond. Several of the women were smoking, and a thick smog hung in the condemned rafters. With a sudden agonizing feeling of constriction, Baba jerked herself upright.

'I want to get out of here,' she said loudly and clearly.

'Sssh!' The woman on her left looked disapproving. 'We're making preparations. Can't you see that?'

But Noreen, on Baba's other side, smiled in sympathy. It was clear that she too had no intention of staying in the church all day.

'Preparations for what?' Baba asked crossly. 'Excuse

41

me please.' And she rose to her feet with a determined expression; Noreen would almost certainly follow.

'To get to the other side, of course,' the woman hissed. 'How do you think you're going to get there if Medea doesn't help you over?'

'The other side?' Baba yawned in spite of herself. 'Why—what happens there?'

Before the woman could answer, a great hush that seemed louder than the singing and chanting which had preceded it swept through the congregation. All the women fell to their knees. Baba was dragged down by Noreen. With a little moan of sadness, she watched a ladder in her tights run swiftly up past the knee.

'Sisters!'

Medea, so tall now in the pulpit that her head seemed to disappear in the swirling mists of brown smoke, had become more a voice than a presence: a black voice that filled the church and echoed in the organ pipes with a booming sound that was truly terrifying.

'Sisters, we are preparing ourselves to reach the Other Side. There will be tribulations, as our oppressors will try to stop us. But let me tell you what awaits us there. A matriarchal society. More than equal pay and educational opportunities. Liberation from childbirth and childcare.'

That's odd, Baba thought sleepily. How can you have a matriarchal society, if that means the mothers running things, and not have children? But her brain hardly felt capable, in such conditions, of dealing with the problem. So far, she thought, it didn't sound particularly tempting on the other side.

'A chance to develop our personalities to the full,' Medea chanted.

'Serious subject—not sex object.

'And abandonment of our sex roles.'

At these words, Baba felt a sort of sadness creep over her. Surreptitiously she felt for her little bunny tail, which had become so ragged and forlorn now, and wondered if it would be possible to get back to the Playboy and ask for a replacement. And as for her ears! They were flopping all over the place. She must look a real mess.

As if she had read her thoughts, Noreen placed an affectionate hand on Baba's knee. 'It'll be all right,' she whispered. 'We'll get out of here.'

It didn't take long for the opportunity to present itself. But it was hardly as Baba would have wished it. In the great silence, with the women on their knees, eyes closed and hardly breathing it seemed, and the soft rushing sound of Medea's voice playing over them like wind pumped from a bellows, footsteps could be heard coming closer and closer to the church, and then stopping in the vestibule outside.

All the women opened their eyes and listened. There was something both strange and familiar about the footsteps. Something sinister, too; several of the women shifted uncomfortably, and for a time Medea's message was lost.

Baba glanced over her shoulder apprehensively. Noreen was frowning and chewing her finger. 'I know what that sound reminds me of,' she hissed at Baba finally. 'It's—it's stiletto *heels*! Isn't it?' she added as half the congregation looked round and nodded agreement. 'What's someone wearing stiletto heels doing *here*, for God's sake?'

Even Medea, at this point, was forced to break off and stare ahead of her at the church door, which was opening slowly. The rushing sound which accompanied her prophecies died away and an expectant silence, as at the beginning of a play, filled the hall. Baba suspected that the women were relieved at the break.

What came round the ancient oak door was a head so apricot blonde, sheepswool curly, heavily rouged, eye-lined and beauty-spotted, that a gasp came up from the audience at the sight. Memories of magazine covers before the Crack—that was only a few days ago, but the event had made the past seem an eternity away—swam before the eyes of the astonished women. Hands dived into shoulder bags for forgotten powder compacts. Tiny tubes of eye-shadow spilled out their iridescent contents on roughened palms. Noreen, with a sigh of envy, simply sat back and stared at the apparition.

Stiletto heels went clack-clack on the worn stone floor of the church. A tent coat in deep plum swung proudly out to either side so that the women felt the rich stuff brush their faces. A leather handbag, with its little lock and golden key, dangled provocatively from creamed, sharp-nailed hands.

'A real 'Fifties Woman,' Noreen whispered piercingly in Baba's ear. 'What d'you think can have happened?' Then her mouth fell open in a circle of disbelief and excitement. 'Are we time travellers?' she gasped. 'Are we back in the 'fifties now, d'you think?'

The strange woman walked with the same even, disturbing step up to the pulpit and stopped there. Separated by many thousands of years, by spinning galaxies of massage, Silkglo Foundation, nylon negligees—separated by a great rift, on one side of which shimmered the prophetic hair and fighting muscle of Medea, and on the other the depilatories and electric dildoes of the decadent twentieth century—the two women faced each other.

Medea was the first to speak. 'Why do you desecrate our temple?'

Her voice, low as a subterranean stream before it bursts triumphantly out on the parched hillside, sent a shiver of fear down Baba's spine. She clung to Noreen for protection.

Then it was the turn of the visitor to answer. The women, ashamed now of their first instinctive dive into their bags for products forbidden by their priestess, looked on sternly.

'I have come in search of an adulteress,' the shining apparition replied.

The leather bag, deftly opened with the cute key, disgorged papers. Medea, a terrible frown lying across her brow like the incision of a surgeon's knife, bent down from the pulpit and took them with a magisterial air.

'There is an adulteress here,' the stranger repeated.

From beneath the double trim-yourself eyelashes, a pair of artificially glistening eyes went slowly and suspiciously round the church. Baba felt herself beginning to squirm in her seat.

'What can she mean?' she whispered to Noreen. 'What does that word mean?'

Medea handed down the papers. When she spoke, rage as menacing as the promise of thunder lay under every word.

'Sisters! We have here a woman who proposes to

waste our time by speaking of past relations between women and men!'

Contempt, too, was in Medea's voice; and the women cringed at the hard glister that fell on their shoulders from on high.

'We will ask this—this imposter to leave the Temple immediately. And we will resume our preparations for the other side.'

But the small eyes, blinking under their load of mascara and paint, continued to move systematically round the hall. Then they stopped.

Just a second too late, Baba dropped her head. Her ears flopped defensively over her face.

'You!' The stiletto heels rang out like pistol shots on the floor. The women in Baba's pew backed nervously. A perfectly fashioned plastic arm, with freckles gaily painted on it in charming little groups as far as the elbow, extended itself from the hidden hook under the permanently deodorized armpit and groped at Baba's breast. The women gave a moan of fear and disgust.

'A Bunny Girl!' said the scarlet mouth. 'Baba the Bunny Girl!'

From close to it was possible to see the thin thread of metal that held the strange visitor's lips in place, and the minute, complicated mechanism, as fascinating as a Swiss watch, that operated just under the dimple on the chin and kept it winking merrily.

'You are the one I am looking for! Come out, my dear.'

Baba glanced up in terror. A smile, spreading at 1.5 millimetres a second, and accompanied by a brisk ticking from the lower jaws, revealed a mouthful of blinding white teeth. On the flat shelf of pink gum the word Pepsodent advertised the product below in forceful frosted writing.

'Who—who are you?' Baba stammered.

Medea's words went unheard once more as the entire congregation craned towards the extraordinary mechanical woman.

'My name is Rene Mangrove,' it said.

The papers were held aloft and Baba shrunk back from them.

'Divorce,' Simon Mangrove's wife intoned. 'Sign the confession statement.'

Clasped in the iron fingers which lay under the velvety skin of the A1 skin graft was a golden fountain pen. The bland brow, unaccustomed to expressions of wonderment or surprise, set itself into a sweet little pattern of wrinkles.

'Get out of here while you can!' Noreen hissed. 'Go on! Now!'

Baba found herself on her hands and knees under the pew. Strong arms pushed her along the floor. She crawled, half conscious with fear, towards the shaft of soupy brown light that poured under the door.

'Alimony!' came the grating, toneless voice after her. 'Sign here please. Sign the confession statement now please.'

'Sisters!' Medea broke in with a great reproachful boom. 'I command you!'

But by this time Baba had reached the open air, and safety, and was running as fast as her legs would carry her in the direction of the river.

8

Baba Goes into the Common Market

The first person to spy Baba running in panic down Cheyne Walk was Joshua McDougall, who had just a few hours before been rescued from his living tomb in the hall of Sir Max Bowlby's house. All Bowlby's guests—the ladies had jumped from the windows on to bedding—were now rehoused in the empty but stately mansion of Pierre Courvoisier, a Common Marketeer who liked to boast of his possessions on both sides of the Channel. A Frenchman by birth and upbringing, Courvoisier brewed his own English ale as proof that the great traditions of the cognac family in no way impaired his anglomania.

Bowlby and McDougall had made an extensive tour of the lopsided but still elegant eighteenth-century home, had forced down the almost undrinkable beer, and were now resting in the front garden, which ran at a sharp angle down to the cracked road and the evil fumes of the drained river-bed.

'Just look at that,' McDougall said feebly. 'A rabbit. Running past.'

Bowlby was too inured by now to feel sorry for his rival in the property field. He knew well that if his own front hall had not removed McDougall's reasoning powers, the shark-like creature would probably have been out and about by now, offering to buy up the ruins.

'A rabbit in some distress,' McDougall went on. 'Let's call it in.'

'Or shoot it?' suggested Pierre Courvoisier from behind them. Only his strong sense of duty and determination to sign up for an enormous shipment of Norman cider had kept him in London over the weekend. He thought sourly of his wife and children enjoying themselves in the country—protected by rolling acres from the rumble of foreign tankers—and, not for the first time, he cursed the fact that his English country-house was in Wiltshire, south of the river. Why had he not gone *nord*, to *la belle Écosse*?

'It *is* a rabbit,' Bowlby said suddenly. It was a relief to be able to see something through Courvoisier's binoculars instead of the maddening obscurity of the opposite bank. 'Yes, Peter, why not get a bit of sport? Keep your gun here?'

Courvoisier said he did. Impervious to the moans of displeasure from the ladies, he staggered out into the hanging garden with a Purdy twelve-bore in hand and a deerstalker on his head. Carefully, he took aim.

'Funny thing,' McDougall said in the thin, crushed voice Bowlby found so irritating. 'That chap Courvoisier was still sweating over his cider shipment this morning. You'd think all this would have rattled him a little. Besides—'

'The sign of a good marketeer,' Bowlby snapped. 'Imperturbable.'

'Besides,' McDougall went on, 'who's he going to sell the stuff to?'

'What?'

A blast from the gun set the drunken lamp-posts in Cheyne Walk swaying. A pigeon, already killed by fallen masonry, exploded into a welter of feathers and blood.

McDougall spelt it out. 'There's no one left to drink the rotten juice. You see what I mean?'

Baba, hearing the gunfire, dived under a newly formed hedge of tree-roots and turf and yellow bricks that once had been the Old Age Pensioners' Garden at the corner of Old Church Street. How sad, she thought, tears starting to her eyes as she saw the stiff paws of terriers and poodles sticking out from under the rubble. I don't mind anything so much as pets being badly treated. What a beastly war this is!

Nevertheless, Baba was determined to get back to the Playboy Club and get fitted out again. It didn't matter how long it took—or how many miles of dangerous enemy territory she had to cross. She would wait for weeks if necessary, hoping to come across a buried food store or hamburger stall on her way. So when she heard firing, she settled herself in quite comfortably by the roots of a memorial cherry tree, closed her eyes, and tried to relax. So long as that terrifying woman didn't find her here—but after all, she was well protected. Baba's ears fell forward and she slept.

'I can see the other side perfectly well,' Lady Bowlby announced. She put down Courvoisier's binoculars and assumed a smug expression. Courvoisier, in a foolhardy but thrusting manner, was exploring the Crack itself after his unsuccessful shooting expedition, and was shouting back inaudible reports to the house.

'I can hear messages too,' Lady Bowlby added. She

gazed mystically at her husband. 'Aren't you interested in what's going on over there, Max?'

'Of course I am, darling.' Bowlby was looking around him with fresh eyes. Like sodden banknotes, the crumpled houses of Chelsea and Knightsbridge lay before him. He glanced thoughtfully at McDougall's invalid form, wondering how much the man had worked out already. It had been obvious to him, perhaps, that the combination of the Fair Rents bill and Courvoisier's high Common Market prices would force the population north of the Thames to seek cheaper accommodation—to go out in the country and grow their own vegetables, even. And that meant a remarkable opportunity for development. Bowlby's mind raced.

'I can see Cars,' Lady Bowlby said portentously, taking up the binoculars again. 'Can you, my dear?' She handed the glasses to the heiress, who was still in a state of shock.

'Oh, yes.' The heiress gave a little sigh of pleasure. She called for her weedy husband and pointed out the orderly stream of traffic that could be descried on the opposite bank.

'Looks like the sort of simple but luxurious big car we've been looking for for years,' the weedy husband said longingly. 'Who can they belong to, I wonder?'

As the dim shapes of the cars swam before the eyes of the heiress and her husband, Courvoisier was wading farther and farther out towards the ever-widening Crack.

The mud, so far, was the consistency of chocolate mousse and came only up to the ankle. All the expected objects were lying in it, some looking pathetic and some disgusting, depending on the upbringing of the viewer. Courvoisier trod carefully, aware that a slip and fall into this mire would mean a lingering death from typhoid. And the hospitals may not be in good shape, he reminded himself grimly. It was important to remember that this expedition—not attempted yet by any of the survivors of the cataclysm—was more momentous even than Captain Scott's. With what tales would he return to his house, where Bowlby and McDougall relaxed indolently, drinking his sherry and planning, in all probability, a property coup to end them all! What if he never did return? Courvoisier searched in his pocket for pen and paper. The last diaries of Captain Courvoisier Cook— and in his mind's eye he saw a hard-cover edition, leather of course, with a golden tassel for a marker.

But in this case the roles of explorer and explored were reversed. For as Courvoisier put a foot forward, his heart thumping and his brain churning out the nineteenth-century language needed to describe the exploit, the Crack visibly and horribly moved towards him.

Courvoisier put his foot back where it had just come from. He had never known, even at the business meetings where he had been impelled to explain his High Prices policy, such a sensation of impending danger.

And the strangest thing about the movement of the Crack was that it appeared to be horizontal. He could see it split like the inane smile on the face of a baby all the way from Battersea Bridge, which lay helplessly across it now, to Southwark. The air was filled with an unpleasant tearing sound which reminded Courvoisier of failed essays of his youth. He looked nervously back at his house, which still bowed deferentially over the river-bed.

Baba was woken from a dream in which two giants, one of them with the sepulchral face of Medea Smith and the other made up of the component parts of Rene Mangrove, fought with each other to the death and finally succeeded in tearing each other apart.

She opened her eyes with a start, to find her legs dangling over the edge of a newly formed crater. A labyrinth of twisted sewage pipes lay below, and she could have sworn she heard the scuffle of rats. With a gasp of horror, she drew back from the jagged invitation to death. If she had slept on …

Lady Bowlby withdrew her chair from the chasm with an exclamation of disgust and moved higher up the slanting lawn with her paraphernalia of binoculars, handbag and chocolates stolen from Pierre Courvoisier's library.

'I knew he shouldn't have gone out there,' she said, angrily gesturing in the direction of the Frenchman. 'He's meddling. Upsetting the balance of nature. And now look what he's done.' She peered out at the river-bed. 'My God. What's that now?' she went on. 'Max. Max!'

As Lady Bowlby's tremulous voice rang out, Baba ran past and disappeared from sight amongst the boulders of the fallen Embankment. Scrambling down the slabs of torn concrete, she found herself on a primeval beach. Oil and soft mud the colour of French mustard covered her feet, and a strange chill ran up Baba's legs, causing her to tuck her tail between her legs for comfort. She looked desperately ahead. On the far bank, the large grey cars moved monotonously. By the edge of the Crack, a man was measuring the depth of the soil with what seemed to be an old chair-leg. From time to time he straightened and made an entry in a small notebook. Grunts of satisfaction wafted back from him to where Baba stood.

An explorer! A real English gentleman explorer! With a warm flood of relief, Baba waded out to meet Courvoisier. He would look after her! She wondered, inspecting his keen back and square, eager shoulders if he might by some miraculous chance be an old client of hers at the Playboy.

Bowlby and McDougall had just finished their little talk in the study. Traversing the one-in-four gradient of the study floor with difficulty, Bowlby went out in answer to his wife's cries. But he paused at the doorless threshold of the room for one last reassuring word. 'That's a deal then, Joshua,' he said.

'It is definitely in our interests to trade with the other side,' McDougall agreed. 'Our initial problem, of course, will be access.'

'A bridge,' Sir Max said impatiently.

McDougall gave a faint smile, but said nothing. From the expression on his face, Bowlby wondered if the crushing he had received the previous evening had really affected his brain. Yet his business acumen seemed as sharp as before.

'For a bridge,' McDougall drawled, 'you need workers. Isn't that right, Bowlby?'

'Max! Max!' came from the garden.

Bowlby shrugged irritably. Was McDougall anticipating trouble with the unions? And who said there were any unions left, after a disaster on this scale? Who could tell, for that matter, if there was anyone left except themselves and the owners of all those cars on the other side? For all one knew—

It only hit Bowlby, when he had slid on his stomach down the marble hall and out into the garden, that if there was no one left he was in trouble indeed. It was hard to envisage a world without workers. But surely, he thought with a spurt of confidence, there must be plenty of workers on the other side.

When Courvoisier saw Baba, in spite of his geological investigations and the new spirit of adventure that was so like his happy days in the nursery, a blissful smile spread across his face.

A beautiful girl was coming towards him through the mud. The Venus of the drained river-bed, a nymph in fishnet tights with sweet little ears and tail that reminded Courvoisier of the Beatrix Potter books in his château nursery.

Her hair was long and pale gold. Black lashes fluttered demurely on her cheeks. Courvoisier forgot his wife and children and stepped backwards through the cloying detritus to meet her.

'I'm Baba,' she said. 'Haven't I seen you somewhere before?'

9

Thirsk Shows Doubt, but Leads His Children into Safety

It took Thirsk and Harcourt, exhausted as they were, several hours to retrace their footsteps from the river to St George's Hospital. They stopped from time to time at a ruined pub, pulling with their last strength pints of draught bitter from behind the counters and drinking the beer in silent gloom amidst the debris of old cigarette ends and crisp packets.

There was every sign that the pubs had been evacuated suddenly—banquettes and beer-stained table swere strewn with bricks and rubble. Half-finished drinks stood on the bar. Coats still hung by the door. Abandoned handbags lay on the seats; and in one pub a poodle was tied to the leg of a chair.

The sun, as brown as the thick clouds that had covered it, plunged the landscape into a state of monochrome, and Thirsk and Harcourt, as they sat holding their glasses on the wooden benches, looked like figures in an early sepia photograph of Victorian London.

They were in a pub off Belgrave Square. Only one more effort was needed to reach St George's.

Thirsk sighed heavily. 'I don't know,' he said as Harcourt looked at him inquiringly. 'I don't know.'

This was the first time in his professional life that

Thirsk had made such a statement and Harcourt goggled at him.

'Where are all the people?' Thirsk said with exasperated patience. 'They shirked, Harcourt.'

'Shirked?' wondered Harcourt.

'They were in great need,' Thirsk said with another heavy sigh. 'And they resisted.'

Harcourt, understanding at last, sighed in sympathy. 'If they had gone into analysis, this would never have happened.'

'If they had regressed,' Thirsk corrected him sternly. 'Imagine, a situation like this—half London falls down, a great crack appears in the river—how would a regressing patient deal with it?'

'He'd love it,' trilled Harcourt.

'Exactly. Happy in their exploration of a new environment. An opportunity, without nuclear family relationships, to form new life structures.'

'And think of playing in the mud of the river-bed,' Harcourt enthused.

Thirsk frowned at him and rose with dignity, gathering his robes. 'One thing has become clear,' he pronounced as they made their footsore way to Hyde Park Corner. 'Our place is no longer here. We have a duty to rescue these people. We cannot remain a small fraternity, surrounded by ignorance and hostility.'

Thirsk puffed out his cheeks as he spoke and Harcourt looked up at him anxiously. 'But there's no one here to be ignorant or hostile,' he ventured.

'We need to be in a place which vaunts its sanity, but is under the surface a society dying of disease,' Thirsk went on. His voice was dreamy, as always, when he launched into what was known to his followers as the Thirsk manifesto.

Harcourt gulped. 'Do you mean the States?' he asked doubtfully.

'I mean—' Thirsk, in spite of his lacerated feet, increased his pace '—I mean, of course, Harcourt, the Other Side.'

Envisaging the old-fashioned mental hospitals crammed with victims of the Crack and receiving shock treatment for their disorders, Harcourt shuddered.

Thirsk's voice broke into his unpleasant reverie. 'Here we are, Harcourt. Let us pray that our children haven't been too badly treated in the oppressive situation in which we left them. The patients—unregressed and unreconstructed as they are—'

It was clear to both analysts, as they approached St George's, that they had nothing to fear on that score. The top storey of the hospital, once the main operating theatre and now used by Thirsk's children as a picnicking site, was blazing merrily, Ned and Mary's barbecue having got out of control almost as soon as it started. From the ground, with whoops of joy, the children trained hosepipes on the coiling flames. Terrified heads poked out of the windows on the floor beneath and a cry for help went up when Thirsk and Harcourt were seen advancing.

'Fire and the father complex,' Thirsk mused as the drew nearer. 'Interesting.'

'A doctor! There's a doctor coming!' cried one misguided cardiac case from the terminal ward. 'Get us out of here, doctor!'

'What shall we do?' Harcourt asked nervously. Since childhood, he had feared fire.

On seeing their true father, the children shrieked with excitement and lowered their hose-pipes to run towards him. A powerful jet of water struck Thirsk in the eye and he staggered for a moment, blinded by the impact.

Dribbling and cooing, Mrs Withers crawled over the furrowed road and grabbed at Thirsk's hem. Ned and Mary, strong and brawny as they were, almost knocked their healer over in their enthusiasm at the reunion. Only Jo-Jo wailed in his surprisingly low-pitched voice in a push-chair by the entrance to Casualty Admissions. Even the fire overhead failed to excite him. His attempts at breast-feeding had brought him frustration rather than fulfilment.

'We get them out of here,' Thirsk said with his old firmness. He pointed in the direction of Hyde Park. 'A quick session there under the trees. And then we make for the river.'

'But the patients?' said Harcourt.

'These are our patients,' Thirsk replied. 'We are responsible for them. And it is our duty to find more. I told you that.'

'I see.' Harcourt looked up once more at the craning heads above. The fire, gaining momentum now, made a tapestry of scarlet and orange against the brown sky. Tying hospital sheets together, several women from the maternity ward began to descend, their babies strapped to their backs.

'Let's go quickly,' Thirsk said in an impatient tone. 'We don't want to be lumbered with unsolicited patients, for Christ's sake.'

10

Another Unfortunate Love Affair for Baba

Baba and Pierre Courvoisier stood for a moment gazing at each other. Then Courvoisier reached out and put his arms round Baba's waist. They drew close together, their feet sinking gently into the soft mud. A half-submerged baby's rattle clung to Baba's leg. As they kissed, the bright ruins of Albert Bridge danced before their eyes.

For Courvoisier, everything was forgotten in the ecstasy of the moment. The Common Market, and his ambitious scheme to bring luxury foods to the rich at special bulk prices. His long-nosed English wife, who had been such a help in his career. His Wiltshire and Garonne estates where he liked to survey the acres and feel at peace with himself. All was forgotten—for Baba.

And for her, the past melted and disappeared, a meaningless succession of disappointing romances. Simon Mangrove, whom she would have been foolish enough to marry if the bumper cars had not luckily intervened, meant no more to her now than her first fiancé, the idiot son of a supermarket millionaire who had spent all his money at the Playboy and was now incarcerated in an asylum somewhere in the North. In between was a row of faceless men who had wanted Baba for her tail and ears, and nothing else. And Baba could tell that Pierre—

explorer, romantic and protective father-figure—loved her for herself. Life was beginning anew. For Baba, the Crack had brought happiness.

Courvoisier's hand tenderly pulled at the bunny outfit. It gave way easily and soon Baba was standing naked before him. In spite of the brown fog, which meant that without binoculars it would be almost impossible for the people on shore to see her, she blushed. These were unusual circumstances—but all the same Baba preferred to undress in the privacy of a bachelor flat.

Courvoisier kissed the small white breasts, which looked like water lilies growing in a muddy pond.

'My beautiful Baba,' he murmured. 'The world comes to an end and you are born. My spotless virgin—my goddess.'

Baba shivered slightly in the dank air. For a moment it crossed her mind that the river-bed might be infested with terrible and contagious diseases. Then she remembered that this, surely, was what an explorer's wife had to put up with all the time. She smiled bravely.

'Where did you come from and where will you lead me?' moaned Courvoisier as he drew Baba closer into his arms. With his left hand he pulled at his trousers until they fell into the mire round his ankles. Overhead a seagull screeched as it flapped its way over the strange new landscape.

Courvoisier pressed his member into Baba with a snort of triumph that sounded like a gun going off. For a time, oblivious of the gently widening Crack and the ominous wavelets of mud that lapped now just below their knees, the lovers lived only for themselves.

'Where will you lead me?' Courvoisier sighed when he

had done. Separate again, he and Baba stood hand in hand only a few feet from the edge of the Crack. He was still, satisfied: but Baba could feel ambition and energy working in him once more. Dazed, she stood beside him and felt his mind race with plans for the future. At last she turned to him tentatively. 'Where were you thinking of going?' she asked.

Courvoisier, as if he had already forgotten her existence, turned to her with a preoccupied air. 'Going?' He dropped her hand to make an expansive gesture. 'I'll tell you, my dear girl, where I was going. To the other side, of course. I, Pierre Courvoisier, am to be the first man to reach the other side. To bring back reports of conditions. To set up a further and more exhaustive expedition.'

His eyes softened as he saw Baba's anxious expression grow. 'With my Baba,' he added. 'Never fear, Baba, if wild and strange people are found there. Pierre will care for you. And if I fall sick, you will care for me.'

With a wince of distaste, Courvoisier hitched his muddy trousers up to his waist. 'We must lose no time,' he said briskly. He pulled a length of rope from the pocket of his suit. 'I took the precaution of bringing this with me. And I will jump first. You, Baba, will hold this rope. And don't—' he gave a heroic smile '—let go, will you? That's a girl.'

'Jump?' cried Baba. 'But Pierre, look at the distance!'

It was true that while they were making love the Crack seemed to have grown several yards. Courvoisier paled, then shrugged.

'Don't go,' Baba pleaded. 'I'll never see you again if you do. And just when we'd found each other, too!'

Tears ran down Baba's cheeks. Having fallen in the

course of the passionate love-making, she was now entirely covered in mud, and only her face, small and pinched with worry, stood out white against the slime brown of her body.

It also occurred to Baba that there was a terrible similarity between Pierre Courvoisier and Simon Mangrove. Perhaps it applied to all men—they couldn't leave danger alone. They had to show off. Remembering Mangrove's death, she began to sob loudly. All men were the same.

Courvoisier, for the first time, began to waver. Was it sensible to leap without proper equipment? This, unlike his Common Market activities, affected him and not the rest of mankind. And he had just fallen in love. He stood back for a moment and considered.

'I'm being chased,' Baba whispered to him. 'A woman —I don't know what she's made of—she's trying to kill me! I promise, it's the truth!'

Courvoisier, his confidence returning, smiled on her benignly. 'A woman? You don't know what she's made of?'

Rapidly and finally, he decided to jump. Poor Baba was clearly a little affected mentally by yesterday's catastrophe. On the other side, they could start a new life. On the other side, untouched by the Bowlbys and McDougalls, who, Courvoisier always felt, made a mockery of his internationalism and brought the country a bad name, they could live innocently and happily together.

Baba felt Courvoisier's decision and reflected with a speed that left her almost exhausted. She grabbed at his arm and looked earnestly up at him.

'Pierre,' she sighed. 'I think at this time you should tell

me something about yourself. I mean—' she gulped, Courvoisier was looking forbidding now '—I mean, you're not *married*, are you?'

Courvoisier flinched. It was true that if he reached the other side he might well find his wife there, and his children. He pictured their faces as he waded ashore, the naked and mud-clothed Baba trailing behind him. If, in Wiltshire, they had heard news of this extraordinary disaster …

'I can tell you are,' sobbed Baba. 'I'm not coming.'

And why shouldn't they have heard news of it, Courvoisier thought grimly. They would have jumped on the first train from Salisbury—the train would have ground to a halt, the driver scratching his head in perplexity as he jammed on the brakes just before Waterloo Bridge. His head shot sharply to the left. Waterloo Bridge, or what was left of it, was invisible from here. Suppose the driver hadn't been able to stop in time … He saw the twisted coaches, their occupants crushed and lifeless, lying in the thick mud of the river-bed.

Love and concern for his wife and family flooded through Courvoisier and left him motionless. Then he pulled himself together. These adventures were part of life. Baba was a wonderful girl. Yet it was his code that wife and family came first.

Baba stepped back dejectedly towards the overthrown embankment. The piece of rope Courvoisier had given her hung from her hands. For the first time she realized that her bunny outfit had sunk irretrievably into the mud. A surge of grief and resignation descended on her, and she felt that never again would she be as unhappy as this. Only one thing remained firmly in her mind. She must reach the Playboy and get fitted out again. And she must at all costs avoid the deathly Rene Mangrove.

'Baba! Come here!' Courvoisier had made up his mind to jump and nothing would stop him. There was no reason, though, to leave Baba behind. Didn't plenty of men have mistresses? And he a Frenchman! He must have been affected, too, by the Crack, to imagine a pure new life with a Bunny girl when his wife was possibly in danger on the other side. Once he had settled her comfortably ... he saw a sweet little flat for Baba somewhere in Clapham, with a comfortable home for himself and his wife in Battersea. Better make sure we're as near the river as we can manage, he muttered to himself. When all this gets sorted out, the riverside houses are bound to go up in value. He had always wanted to live on the Left Bank.

Courvoisier tugged impatiently on the rope and Baba felt herself dragged back to his side. Like a lamb to the slaughter, she thought sadly as she stumbled towards him.

'Darling!' Courvoisier bestowed a last, meaningful kiss. 'Hold the rope firmly, and then I'll pull you over! You know I can't live without you.'

Baba shrugged. A numb indecision seemed to have come over her and she stood uncertainly on the edge of the Crack. Perhaps, if he really wanted her ...

Courvoisier jumped.

The brown fog enveloped him almost at once but Baba, her eyes scanning the horizon, could just make out long cars with fins like sharks cruising peacefully on the other side. Perhaps it would be all right there after all ...

The rope ran out through Baba's fingers. An impossible

weight jerked her face down into the mud. The echoing cry that rose from the Crack brought a flock of seagulls, hysterically circling the waterless river, to flap and scream above.

With a last wrench, the rope flew out of Baba's hands and slid into the mouth of the Crack.

The reverberations of the shout died away. The seagulls, no longer curious, flew upstream in search of rotting fish. Baba, her eyes staring in terror from her brown face, struggled back to shore.

11

The Fate of Ballooning Liberals

Jeremy Waters worked hard, his fingers trembling with impatience. It was clear to him now that if he and his family reached the other side, they would at last find the life which he had hoped to find in Hampstead.

At last, a society in which ecology and socialism went hand in hand. A society of brothers, fighting together to preserve the strange and beautiful structures thrown up by the Crack, and treating each other with decency and respect.

Communism without a dictatorship! And the worst of it was that Waters might be too late. Everyone else had got there first.

He trembled to think of what had got going there in his absence. State Capitalism, perhaps. Or plain old-fashioned capitalism, with notorious evil-doers like Sir Max Bowlby and Joshua McDougall in control of the town planning. Aided and abetted by a Fascist like Pierre Courvoisier, the Common Marketeer—Waters gritted his teeth as he toiled on, putting the finishing touches to the vehicle which would carry them safely across.

He had heard the news of the Crack from his son's transistor radio. A sinister, chilling woman's voice had announced after hours of vacuous pop music:

The river is exhausted, the banks are wide,
A new life for women on the Other Side.

And he had risen from his trance of fear at the foot of the new Nash Acropolis to find that his mission awaited him and he might well be too late for it!

Not that Waters saw himself as a saviour. But after all his father had fought in the Spanish Civil War. His great-uncle had gone to Russia in 1919 and come back with an entirely new life-style, freeing his butler and housemaids from serfdom. An ancestor on his mother's side had been a Tolpuddle martyr. It was clearly Waters's duty, as the revolutionary intellectual he had trained himself to be, to reach the masses and show them the light.

The balloon was nearly ready. Life-jackets from the crashed Jumbo provided ballast. Dead stewardesses' skirts, stitched together by the patient Mrs Waters, waited for the wind. The body of the vessel, which had caused the most trouble, was made up out of carefully assembled portions of fuselage. A kitbox in the pilot's cabin had supplied glue and nails.

'It's nice to think,' Waters remarked as he worked happily, 'that the simple necessity—the nail, the pot of glue—is still to be found on board one of these giants of a technological age. And, thanks to these early inventions, we shall soon be airborne.'

'There's no wind,' Waters's son pointed out.

Little enthusiasm had been shown by the family for the expedition. Even Waters's wife, with all the blandishments of a new life for women on the other side, had shown a stubborn refusal to look optimistically into the future.

'Pessimism of the will, optimism of the intellect, darling,' Waters breezed. 'I only hope that when we get there we won't find ourselves too hopelessly individualistic.'

Waters refrained from voicing his real fears. After all, if they found fascism on the other side they could always get into the balloon and take off again. But he knew he had to fight the Robinson Crusoe in him. It would be only too easy to settle down here in Regent's Park, welcome the odd lame duck who had failed to get there to join their commune, and be out of the main course of history altogether. And then who would remember him? Sweating, he worked on.

It seemed as if providence was on their side. After twenty-four hours of a brown, windless sky, dispelled a little by the rays of the sun but sluggish and humid to the point of being unbearable, a delightful little breeze got up just as the balloon was completed.

He lit a fire from driftwood and the Cardin skirts filled out with hot air and billowed proudly. As the wind grew in force the vehicle moved slightly on the ground, as if impatient to be off. Waters stood back and smiled. He turned to his family, who were sitting in attitudes of dejection amongst the crushed tulips. The wind tugged at their clothes and moaned in the fallen masonry of the Nash terraces.

'That's what I heard before,' Waters pronounced. 'That great rushing sound. Remember?'

He knew as he spoke that the rushing sound had been something terrible and supernatural, and not the wind at all—but again there was no point in encouraging despondency. Everything should seem as normal as possible.

With resigned, defeated expressions the Waters family climbed aboard the balloon. The wind had reached gale force by now. Waters, with the gay air of a paterfamilias at a coconut stall, threw out a handful of life-jackets.

The balloon rose with a sudden life of its own.

Several of the children and step-children gave cries of delight. Waters smiled kindly. It was almost too good to be true—they were high above Regent's Park already and had a splendid view of the new London. The B.B.C. building had collapsed into the street: Waters found himself suppressing a smile of pleasure. If only they had accepted his demands to speak on their programmes, to warn of the dangers that lay ahead for mankind! They had invariably chosen pseudo-scientists who had put the problem in far too far-reaching terms. And look at them now! He hoped piously that they had been able to get out alive.

A moment of sadness came with the sight of Billings and Edmonds, where he had been fitted out for private school, no more than a pile of rubble on the ground. And Simpson's! Waters glanced down at his suit and told himself sternly that these were the feelings he must guard against. If necessary, the spinning and weaving skills he and his wife had cultivated in Hampstead would be taught to the masses on the other side.

When they passed over Jermyn Street and Savile Row, however, Waters averted his gaze. Burlington House still stood—thank heavens for that! He wondered vaguely about the National Gallery and the Tate.

Then the direction of the wind changed.

The balloon turned violently to one side, spilling out the family spaniel and discarding the remaining ballast. With a sickening heave they rose higher and higher until they were engulfed by wet clouds. London was no longer visible below. And the wind became whimsical, tossing the frail vessel first in one direction and then another. It seemed, to Waters's fear-crazed brain, to have taken on a life of its own, and to be teasing them with its hidden intentions. Waters thought of the bully at his school thirty years before: a slight lull would be followed by a vigorous shaking; a moment of hope by torment more awful than anything that had preceded it.

Mrs Waters looked at her husband timidly. 'Are we crossing now?' she asked. Accustomed to rough Channel crossings, she folded her hands and looked with resignation down at her stomach. Waters could be strangely unsympathetic when she was sick.

'I like it up here!' the youngest Waters child cried. 'Can we stay up here for ever, Daddy?'

As if in reply to this foolish question, the wind gave a succession of brisk puffs, which reminded Waters of a cherub with his cheeks blown out, a picture that had always entranced him in his nursery. In between the puffs was a sinister stillness—and each time the balloon fell at least twenty feet, only to be buoyed up again before it was too late. Mrs Waters, retaining her gracious poise, was sick over the side.

A great puff swept them once more sideways in a movement that was oddly like skating on a rink made of air. Then the wind dropped. They went down fast. Waters managed a sickly smile, meant to be reassuring. They went faster—the brown clouds thinned, the tops of trees came at them like spears—the grassy earth bulged out to meet them.

12

Waters Sees his Reflection

When the balloon hit the Serpentine, a flock of naked bathers scattered like flamingoes on to the muddy banks. Putrid water rose in a fan and drenched the Waters as they lay stunned in the belly of their amateurish vehicle.

On tiptoe, the naked men and women peered in at them. Then they began to laugh. The laughter was mad and babyish, as if an infant were being tickled to the point of hysteria.

Waters closed his eyes immediately after opening them. From the thick lips of one of the men hung a much-chewed baby's rattle. A woman of about forty with straggling grey hair was blowing her nose on the back of her hand and rubbing it vigorously on Mrs Waters's blouse. Several of the bathers were crying and moaning with laughter—and in some cases a real crying fit ensued. Worst of all, a trickle of urine ran down the leg of a mournful-looking woman who stood, thumb in mouth, at a short distance from the others.

So this was the new paradise!

Waters gritted his teeth and pulled himself to a half-sitting position. Rousseau was forgotten. Man in his innocent loveliness, waiting only for the guidance of Waters, presented itself to his horrified gaze.

'Savages!' he groaned.

Slithering down the trampled mud towards them came two black-robed figures. With their long matted hair and heavy, purposeful stride they transported Waters to the nightmares of his childhood, when John the Baptist and Jesus together came to punish him for being naughty. Unconsciously, he prayed for deliverance.

Harcourt and Thirsk stopped as they reached the fringes of their flock.

'A balloon,' Harcourt announced. 'Men from another culture, Joe?'

'A case of womb envy,' Thirsk allowed. He put out a restraining hand as Harcourt was about to dash forward. 'We must remember the new methods of anthropology,' he went on. 'We do not appear on the scene to annotate and classify. We observe, and we appreciate a life-style that does not resemble our own but is nevertheless contemporaneous with it. We do not overlay our post-imperialist value-judgments.'

'Quite so,' Harcourt said faintly. Waters's head and shoulders were just visible in the balloon and he was ashamed to find himself relieved at the fact the man was dressed. So much nakedness had once more caused a longing for order, which only a return to the States could gratify.

'We will not pronounce these people savages, whatever their ritual may be,' Thirsk intoned. 'Incest taboos— cannibalism—'

Waters, catching the word cannibalism, shuddered to his feet in the balloon. Instincts normally denied to late twentieth-century bourgeois man crowded in on his feverish brain. The draft-dodgers he had sheltered in his

Hampstead home were no longer a proud memory. His uncle George, a conscientious objector in the war, seemed now a ludicrous and pathetic figure. Squaring his shoulders, Waters snarled openly across the crowd at Thirsk.

'He's certainly violent,' Harcourt whispered nervously. 'What do we do now?'

Thirsk, who needed violence daily as much as a carnivorous animal needs red meat, bared his teeth in turn at Waters. Thirsk's patients looked wonderingly from one adult to another. Memories of childhood traumas, impossible fights between their parents, aggression towards themselves flooded back. Ned and Mary, who had been in care since the ages of one and two started to scream first.

'Who are you?' Waters shouted over the shrieks. 'Where am I? Is this the other side?'

Thirsk smiled. He said quietly, 'Yes, this is the other side. Welcome, brother. You must forgive the children. They are only expressing themselves. They need a father to vent their pent-up feelings, and I'm afraid the fact you descended from the skies caused the God/Sun king complex to manifest itself.'

Waters gave a bitter smile. Thirsk's speech was familiar—Hampstead was crawling with men like this— and he furiously regretted having been impressed by their theories. He had even bought their books! Once more, he bared his teeth in a snarl.

'We must work together for a new society,' Thirsk went on in his too-reasonable voice. 'And this is my colleague, Nigel Harcourt.'

Without thinking, Waters extended his hand politely.

Another wave of rage overcame him when he saw that such symbols from a dead culture had been discarded and Harcourt only looked him in the eye.

Thirsk's children, amused by Waters's family, started to play housey with the youngest daughter in the roots of a great oak. Peals of laughter drifted towards the adults as the real and artificial children, darting amongst the branches of the fallen tree, exposed themselves to each other and set up fast-changing games of Mummy and Daddy. Mrs Waters, terrified that her children might become corrupted, ran screaming over the grass to put an end to the pre-latency amusements.

Waters took the opportunity to look warily around.

What he saw was Hyde Park. Disbelievingly, he raised his binoculars. It was lucky, he thought with grim satisfaction, that he had had the presence of mind to grab them as he was swept from his Hampstead drawing-room.

In the distance, by the armless Peter Pan statue, a pile of grey-flannelled nannies lay on the ground. Coroneted perambulators heaped behind them, the brightly polished wreckage gleaming in the sun. A handful of babies, their hair still neatly plastered to their heads and their scrubbed faces aglow with pleasure, crawled aimlessly round the bodies of their warders.

There was no doubt about it. The ruined Albert Hall, splendid as the Coliseum, was clearly visible. Millionaire's Row, untouched by the disaster, stood straight and un-ashamed. By adjusting the focus of the powerful binoc-ulars, Waters could see the deserted Derry and Toms roof garden. He turned to Thirsk with a thin smile.

'So this is the other side,' he remarked. 'There doesn't seem to be much originality of design.'

Before Thirsk, who was in the process of realizing that Waters was less inane than he looked, had time to answer, a great scream went up from his patients under the tree. Thirsk, distracted by the sound, decided that for the first time in his life he had better admit his error. It was clear that even he would be unable to contain Waters's righteous rage.

Harcourt, sensing that his master was about to come clean, trembled in his shoes.

The screaming grew louder. Waters, the stronger of the two now, paid no attention to it.

He pulled his son's air pistol from his pocket and aimed at Thirsk. With a cumbersome gesture, Thirsk raised his great arms above his head.

Then Thirsk was saved. Followed by the mob of screaming children, an extraordinary figure was running over the muddy banks of the Serpentine towards them.

It was impossible to tell where the figure began and the mud ended. It seemed, in fact, to be the hideous mockery of a human being made entirely of mud; a living creation of the slime itself. The gun fell from Waters's hand and he crossed himself. As it came nearer, the horribly realistic limbs gesturing in a mad parody of human communication, even Thirsk paled and stepped back, stumbling in the folds of his robe.

But Thirsk was never slow to think. Regaining his composure, he faced Waters and spoke clearly and with contempt.

'Is it not clear to you,' he enunciated as Harcourt gazed up at him with fear and admiration, 'that this is the mirror image of the world we live in? That the people you see here, naked and savage as they are, are the reflections of ourselves? Dehumanized man laid bare: the other side of the self and other?'

Waters, temporarily silenced by Thirsk's conviction and brilliance, felt his tired mind atrophy as the events of the last twenty-four hours overcame him. Wasn't it reasonable enough that the other side would be but the mirror of the side he knew? Was it possible in life to escape yourself by moving away from your environment? He knew well that man carries his ruin with him.

The moving figure of mud ran to within a few feet of where they stood and collapsed in the element whence it had come. A woman! Evil womanhood, dragging man down into the abyss since the beginning of time. Woman symbolized by the primeval slime; all round her the fallen and ruined Garden of Eden. Woman crawling towards them like a serpent on its belly—

With expressions of fastidious disgust, both Waters and Thirsk inched away from the spectacle. Only the children, their gay laughter animating the devilish landscape, pelted the creature with balls of mud and screamed alternately.

'Please,' cried Baba. 'Help me. I'm looking for Park Lane—I'm on my way to the Playboy Club to get fitted out—There's a woman after me—' Baba's hands groped frantically for the hem of Thirsk's robe. Sternly he drew away from her.

'Who are you?' Waters demanded in an inquisitorial tone. To his own shame he found the sight of the mud woman strangely exciting. How could it be that he, Waters, a supporter of the feminists in their claims for equality was provoked to a state of erection by Baba's abasement? Sighing, he supposed that these things were sent as a trial on the Other Side. The suspicion dawned on him that this might in fact be Limbo, where God examined your behaviour before making up His mind where you should go.

'My name's Baba,' the pathetic girl said. 'I'm looking for Park Lane!'

Sobs that were only too human choked through the thick layers of slime. In an agony of embarrassment, Waters attempted to hide with his hand his state of arousal and glanced at Thirsk for support.

Thirsk had noticed. His full power restored, he smiled invisibly behind his beard.

'This is the type of woman who goes on to become the schizophrogenic mother,' he announced. 'The sins of the mothers are handed down through the generations. Our opportunity, in this society at the dawn of creation, is to remove the mother altogether and substitute the communal anti-family.'

As he spoke, Thirsk's mind raced. Whatever happened, he must prevent Waters from crossing the river. He must leave him here, ostensibly in charge of the new society, while he and Harcourt shepherded their children to the other side. What better than to set up a camp for women like this—and Thirsk didn't doubt that the clubs of Soho and the respectable homes of Knightsbridge alike would yield their quota of disastrous women, all of whom would wander into Hyde Park—what better than to suggest to Waters that he stay here in charge of them? Waters was clearly in a state of extreme sexual repression: in the guise of instructing these women in the true path, he could indulge himself to his heart's content. And get on to the first stage of regression at the same time! Thirsk liked to help all mankind.

Baba's shrill voice broke into his calculations. 'Oh God!' she cried. 'Look! She's got here! Help me! Help me!'

The children gave another piercing scream as the new arrival descended on them. This was too good to be true! As Thirsk and Waters's eyes goggled and poor Harcourt covered his face with his hands, a figure more unbelievable than the first came running with odd, mechanical movements over the grass and at full tilt towards Baba's muddy patch. Thirsk's low whistle sounded sibilantly.

'A doll! A doll!' the children shouted. Mary and Mrs Withers rushed at it, all their frustration at their lost playthings expressing itself in a wild possessiveness.

'Rene Mangrove,' moaned Baba. 'Don't let her get at me, whatever happens!'

But there was little chance of that. Before she could reach her goal the life-sized artificial woman had been pulled down by the children and had disappeared in a kicking fray of arms and legs.

Ned and Mary, who had always fought over their toys, tugged at her from either end. A thoughtful bespectacled man, regressing as a long-hoped-for cure for homosexuality, pulled off her skirt and folded it into the shape of a nappy. Before he could change Rene Mangrove, Jo-Jo had seized it from him and torn it to shreds.

Bleached nylon hair came out in tufts and scattered in the breeze like dandelion puffs. A bright blue eye sailed through the air and landed at Thirsk's feet. Metallic lips curved in a love-goddess smile lay forgotten in the mud.

Baba gave a little sigh. 'Everyone I'm connected with seems to come to a bad end,' she said sadly.

A manly feeling came over Waters at the words. Tenderly he helped Baba to her feet. With his own hands he would bathe her in the waters of the Serpentine. With his love he would bring her self-esteem and respectability.

Thirsk summed up the situation and signalled to Harcourt. In the distance, and exhibiting every sign of distress, Mrs Waters was making for her husband at full speed. The woman-doll was no more than a broken toy. The children had abandoned it already.

As Waters stood with his arm round Baba, Thirsk gathered up his flock with the promise of Smarties all round at the end of the journey, and they crept away in the direction of the river.

13

Baba Fights her Way back to the Playboy—Just in Time

Park Lane was deserted except for the animals. It seemed that every pet in London, tired of waiting for the return of its owner, had decided to assemble there.

Baba, escaped from the reforming embrace of Waters, rounded Hyde Park Corner and stopped in her tracks. A phalanx of Securicor Alsatians growled menacingly at the frail mud-caked figure. Coyly aware of their attractions, a small band of trimmed white poodles danced along the road towards her. Escaped pet mice, disoriented by the absence of their toy wheel and breeding box, ran like drifting snow across her feet.

'Oh dear,' sighed Baba. 'Now what am I to do?'

So near, yet so impossibly far stood the imposing building of the Playboy. It was strange, Baba thought as she gazed longingly at the two erect ears still glowing luminously outside it, that the Playboy was the only place not to have suffered in some way from the catastrophe. The top storey of the Hilton—and here she had to admit to a twinge of nostalgia for poor Simon Mangrove —had fallen off completely. The Dorchester had grown extraordinarily thin in the middle and wide at the edges, so that some of the rooms, Baba imagined, must be two feet square now, and others pointlessly distended. As for

Apsley House—but Baba made up her mind not to look back at the smouldering ruins of St George's and the fallen mansion of the Iron Duke. The lucky part was that the Playboy stood firm. And somehow, through this jungle infested by dangerous animals, she had to reach it.

Inside the Playboy, everything went on as it had before. Because of the failure of electricity there was no closed-circuit television, and fiery torches lent an air of late Roman extravagance to the cocktail bar, the Bunny girls resembling some kind of startling mythical animal as they handed round the drinks and waggled their tails for the customers. Otherwise, it would have been impossible to tell that a catastrophe of such proportions had taken place outside.

'What I say is,' remarked Nicholas Ebbing-Smith as he sipped at his fifth Old-fashioned, 'is let them know we're not giving in this time. We can manage without their electricity better than they can manage without our money.'

'Power cuts bring the country down,' Jeremy Potts agreed drunkenly.

'Starve them out.' Ebbing-Smith strengthened his point.

Potts and Ebbing-Smith sat in companionable silence for a time. Potts glared down at his watch and sighed. 'Five o'clock,' he said. 'Another late night, Nick. But what's the use of going to the office when the air-conditioning doesn't work? Think I'll skip it again.'

'I used to envy you, having an office to go to,' Ebbing-Smith confided. Eyes moist, he turned to his friend for sympathy. 'But seeing what a worry it's been to you. I'm pretty glad now I didn't take the plunge.'

'Ulcers,' Potts confirmed. He glanced at his watch again, puzzled. 'Hey, Nick, it can't be five in the morning, you know. It must be—how long *have* we been here, anyway?'

'You mean to say it's the afternoon?' Ebbing-Smith chortled. 'Well, well.'

Although both men laughed, a tiny shadow of fear crept across their faces. In the light from the flares, the bar where they sat seemed suddenly timeless, without beginning or end or geographical existence. The piano tinkled; the girls passed like waves lapping on a beach. Behind the bar, always and mysteriously full, the bottles of scotch and vodka and crème de menthe glinted. The barman's arm rose and fell, an unending martini shaking gently between his hands. Potts and Ebbing-Smith glanced at each other, still pretending to smile.

'Let's go up to the roof,' Ebbing-Smith suggested casually. 'If it's the afternoon it'll do us good to get a breath of air.'

The two men rose and sauntered to the door. To their surprise, they found they were joined almost at once by all the other men in the bar. Only the Bunny girls went mechanically about their business. The piano tinkled on monotonously, unaware of the sudden rush to the exit. 'Great men think alike,' Potts said uneasily.

A heave from the impatient crowd behind them sent Potts and Ebbing-Smith at frantic speed up the stairs. Ignoring the feeble cries of the Playboy visitors who had been in the lift at the time of the electricity cut, they surged out on to the roof.

A deep gasp, like a dog snarling in its sleep, went up

83

from the men as they saw the scene before them. For a moment there was silence.

Then fifty voices started up at the same time. The older customers, some of them still convalescing from prostate operations, clasped themselves and gazed apprehensively up at the skies for signs of Hitler's bombers. The younger men, unprepared by the State for an emergency on this scale, stared in perplexity and horror at the fallen houses and wrecked funfair of Hyde Park.

Below, scenting the presence of humans, the abandoned pets sent up a howl of rage and protest.

'Whatever can have happened?' Ebbing-Smith said. In spite of the lameness of his remark his obvious un-flappability caused several of the more panicky men to cluster round him for support.

'And what's that?' Potts cried. The hysteria in his voice communicated itself to the crowd, which now edged away from their two leaders.

'Air raid,' barked an ex-brigadier amongst them. 'Cover, boys!'

A rushing sound, growing louder and louder, filled the air. Hands over their ears, the terrified men crouched on the Playboy roof. Apart from the fact that half of them thought that the sound heralded the arrival of the Russians and the other half that it was the Chinese, the feelings were unanimous. The end had come. They were all about to die.

A voice—low, chilling, a woman's voice—spoke through the mad whirlpool of racing air. Slowly, trembling with fear, the men uncovered their ears and looked up at the brown clouds above them as they churned across the sky.

The voice seemed to emanate directly from the heavens:

The river is exhausted, the banks are wide,
A new life for women on the Other Side.

The rushing sound died away. Shakily, not liking to catch each others' eyes, the men rose to their feet.

Then another sight, more disturbing to them than the wreckage of Park Lane, caused them to pull their handkerchiefs from their pockets and dab desperately at their brows.

The Bunny girls had escaped out into the street and were running as fast as their legs could carry them down to Hyde Park Corner.

In blind obedience to the voice they ran through the swarming pets and past the muddy, pathetic figure of Baba, who hesitated still amongst the ruins of Les Ambassadeurs. They had to get to the river. They had to find Medea Smith.

Taken aback by the giant rabbits, the dogs and cats and hamsters backed into the park. A short volley of barking went up, but the girls ran on unmoved, their ears flapping as they ran.

A great cry went up from the men on the Playboy roof. And then, the road clear of the menacing animals and the haven of the Playboy only a few blissful minutes away, Baba began to walk quickly and happily towards them. An outfit at last! The life she had missed so much restored to her! She smiled, picking her way carefully over the broken tarmac.

14

The Answer to a Magnate's Prayers

Sir Max Bowlby lay dreaming in the triangular room, once Pierre Courvoisier's master bedroom with bathroom *en suite*. It was now a strange mixture of the two, the contracting walls having pushed the bath up next to the bed and flung the lavatory, a fine Victorian fake of gleaming mahogany and canework, half out of the window so that it overhung the sloping lawns below. The fitted cupboards had bulged and split, and Bowlby lay in an uncomfortable array of Madame Courvoisier's evening dresses, most of which were covered in sharp sequins that nudged him awake just as his dream was at its most reassuring.

He dreamed that everything was back to normal again.

In his office, the blonde secretary was bringing coffee to the dark-haired personal assistant. The multi-phones rang constantly, and as he snapped into the red, green and blue receivers lights flickered on the maps of the Seychelles and the Sardinian hinterland. Imposingly, taking up the entire wall opposite his desk, was the construction plan, in sombre black and white grain of the redevelopment plan for Calcutta. PUT INDIA ON THE MAP stood out in bold lettering under the plan; the best architects had been hired to outdo Brasilia for Bowlby.

On Bowlby's desk was a studio portrait of his wife and his beloved Pomeranian sheepdog. It was six o'clock in the dream, for Bowlby was rising from his desk and stretching his arms with a satisfied expression.

From the wide, curved window it could be seen that everything was normal in London, too.

The rush hour was in full swing, and at the foot of the Bowlby building Bowlby's Bentley and chauffeur waited. A slice of the dome of St Paul's, obscured by empty office blocks and skyscrapers, glinted in the late evening sun. Faces pinched with worry, the blonde secretary and the dark-haired personal assistant hovered at the door of the office. Bowlby knew they hoped to get to the shops before late-night crowds made it impossible for them, and he smiled expansively. It was his last twinge of power before being driven home, sipping at his martini and being driven out again with his wife to a dinner where he would be asked several times to be god-father to the latest arrivals of destitute aristocratic ladies; and, as always, he took advantage of it.

'A letter, Miss Griffiths,' he barked out.

Controlling her despair, the blonde secretary came forward. The phone rang once more: a Tokyo business-man who wanted to set up a casino complex at Lourdes. It was a good idea, Bowlby reflected, outdoing the acrosexbatics at Las Vegas. Cripples and gamblers alike could relax in the healing waters between bouts of roulette and chemin de fer. He grunted approval and hung up.

The secretary crossed her legs provocatively, shorthand pad on lap. Bowlby glanced at the clock, wondered if there was time, before the Duchess of Savage's cocktail party ...

The head of a fox stole on Madame Courvoisier's best winter coat bit deep into Bowlby's shoulder and he woke up. He groaned, swinging his legs over the dusty bath to reach the window, no more than a medieval slit now, of Courvoisier's master bedroom. If only, he thought in desperation as he pushed the ponderous Victorian lavatory to one side and looked out, there could be a crowd of *people* below! A crowd of eager workers, blue-overalled. In his mind's eye he saw the bridge that would carry them across. Delicate, vast: a Tay bridge that needed men permanently on it, painting and repairing. And he and McDougall—and their wives too, of course—cutting the ribbon at the completion of the bridge, striding, high above the dregs of the Thames, to the great opportunities on the other side.

The bridge, worked on night and day by teams of sweating labourers, would take only a week or so to build. Bowlby's Versailles, his Great Pyramid.

But there was no one to be seen anywhere. An acrid stench from the open cesspit of the river-bed caused Bowlby to reach for Madame Courvoisier's bottle of Chanel No. 5. He dabbed it on to the corner of a sequinned dress and waved it in front of his nose. It was a clear, light morning and the brown clouds had rolled away altogether, leaving a breeze that would have been deliciously refreshing under any other circumstances. Bowlby sighed.

One of his worst troubles in the feverish night he had just spent was a recurring fantasy about a naked, mud-covered girl he had seen running down Cheyne Walk the night before. When he had mentioned the vision to his wife she had only laughed—and to punish her he had insisted she sleep in McDougall's half-destroyed study. Now he felt guilt: he knew she was suffering from bad stomach cramps after a diet of Courvoisier's preserved fruits and Charbonnel and Walker chocolates; and the cold night air must have been extremely injurious to her. But at the same time he was unable to forget the fleeing, muddy figure—the sweet little face, the buttocks like Chanteloup melons as they pumped energy into the slender legs.

Then he gave a hoarse shout. Down on the Embankment, crossing the Royal Hospital Road and looking to the right, the left and the right again at the tortured traffic lights, came a band of people. Their clothes were tattered and they seemed to be waving rattles and blowing toy trumpets, but they were people. Workers! If it seemed strange that they should pay so much attention to the pedestrian code when there were no cars in working order, it mattered little to Bowlby. He wetted his lips and gave another shout.

McDougall, dozing uneasily in his perpendicular library, leapt to his feet. If Bowlby was as excited as this, there must be some major change in prospects. Eyes shining under the brow responsible for so many conversions, he struggled to the door of Courvoisier's house and looked out.

What he saw disappointed him, but McDougall was accustomed to dealing with hippie labourers. With a well-trained eye he totted up the size of the potential work force. Over one hundred men and women! With a sigh of relief he saw the bridge leap and bound across the widening Crack.

He had been about to admit defeat. The fine weather

and good visibility was making the ordered, harmonious life in progress on the other side almost unbearable. Repeated flag-waving and booming through home-made megaphones had been answered only by cryptic and maddening messages in a woman's voice. It had seemed, even to McDougall, that the twenty-first century, beckoning and at the same time repudiating them on the far side of the river-bed had no intention of including such men as himself and Bowlby in it. But now!

Thirsk's children wandered uncertainly down Cheyne Walk. A few moments before, both Thirsk and Harcourt had been with them; now both had disappeared.

'I want my Daddy,' moaned Mrs Withers. She kicked savagely at Jo-Jo by way of reprisal. 'Where's that bastard Daddy gone?'

The other children eyed Mrs Withers with tired hatred and marched on. They dimly remembered the safety of Thirsk's cork-lined clinic, and felt they were nowhere near home here. Only Ned and Mary retained their ebullience, giving a halloo of delight when they saw the oozing playground of mud stretched out before them. The parent figures were forgotten as they ran laughing to the parapet and gazed down through the crumbled cement slabs at the river-bed below.

McDougall seized his opportunity. Without stopping to help Bowlby clamber down from the triangular room he dashed out into Cheyne Walk, his arms laden with gifts. A gasp of delight went up from the children as crystallized violets, Napoleon brandy and brass telescopes were showered down on them. Gratefully they sank on to Courvoisier's steep lawn and ate and drank.

McDougall ran up the lawn, grabbing at tufts of grass

in order not to slip back. Peremptorily, in a tone he had almost forgotten how to use, he ordered Lady Bowlby out of the study and into the remains of the kitchen, where there might still be smoked salmon in the overturned refrigerator. 'Make sandwiches,' he barked. 'Hurry!'

Lady Bowlby, dazed by her bad night and the hostility of Sir Max, stumbled obediently towards the kitchen and collapsed in tears amongst the wreckage of Moffat cooker, dishwasher and severed Wastemaster.

'Really,' she moaned to the collection of useless appliances, which seemed to be regarding her with curious disapproval, 'if I don't get to the other side soon I simply don't know what I shall do!'

15

Baba Sings for the Last Time

Falling in love again
What am I to do?
Never wanted to
I just can't help it.

Baba was in her seventh heaven. In fact, she had to rub her eyes often to convince herself she wasn't dreaming — but the smudge of dark blue mascara and soft iridescent eye-shadow that came off on the back of her hand when she did were enough to show that this really was happening and she wasn't asleep at all.

Here she was, doing her Marlene Dietrich before a crowd of appreciative, applauding men.

She was back in the Playboy, and when she had finished her cabaret turn a brand new bunny outfit awaited her.

Best of all, all the other girls had left. Baba felt she should have warned them that however compelling Medea Smith's voice might sound, they wouldn't enjoy the converted church at World's End. But they had run off too fast. And now Baba was undisputed Queen.

With a final brandish of her top hat, Baba stepped down from the stage. The tinkling piano started up again; the men strolled over to the bar to help themselves to drinks.

The shaker went on shaking. Glacé cherries and olives fell with little plops into iced spirits. Nuts spilled out into dishes and were consumed hungrily.

The men were tired, Baba realized this, but what a perfect life to go on in perpetuity! If they became jaded she regaled them with another number and they soon perked up again. It was just as Baba had always said: the sexual appetite was what counted.

Smiling and bowing, Baba ran off to change into her bunny outfit. The trials and exhaustions of the days since the Crack were already forgotten, and she found she wasn't tired at all. It would be nice, she decided, to serve the next round of drinks herself—then the poor angels wouldn't have to stir themselves. Glowing with happiness and success, she arranged her new tail and gave a pert nod to her head that sent her ears flying.

'What the hell are we going to do?' Ebbing-Smith muttered to his friend Potts. 'If this is a war, why haven't we been captured or something?'

The two men, close since their schooldays and automatically suspicious of any outsider, had been joined by a third man. Smooth dark hair, a slightly sanctimonious smile: he bore all the marks of the type of person most mistrusted by Potts and Ebbing-Smith. In order not to be overheard by him they spoke in choked whispers, glancing pointedly away from him when he seemed about to speak.

> She used to love waltzes
> So please don't play a waltz.
> She danced divinely, and I loved her so.
> But there I go.

croaked the pianist. The Martini shaker, keeping time with the music, rattled monotonously. Ebbing-Smith groaned.

'Excuse me,' the stranger said. 'May I introduce myself?'

Potts stuffed a handful of nuts into his mouth and reached for a cigarette. Ebbing-Smith waved with simulated gaiety at Baba as she came towards them.

'Cornelius,' the stranger persisted. 'Brother Cornelius as a matter of fact. I just happened to be passing, you know, when this ... this cataclysm took place. And ducked in for shelter, you might say.'

'Really? How interesting,' Potts said in a bored voice.

'I never imagined,' the priest gabbled, 'that I'd find Sodom and Gomorrah the only places not destroyed.' He gave a high, excited giggle. 'And I keep hearing voices—messages from the other world—'

Potts and Ebbing-Smith glanced at each other with distaste. This was the last straw: a Roman Catholic priest, of all things, in the Playboy. And every sign of being walled up with him till Judgment Day.

Baba lowered her tray of drinks and waggled her tail.

'A drink, sir?' she murmured to Brother Cornelius. The man had intrigued her while she was doing the number before the Marlene Dietrich—the vamp number in which she stripped down to fishnet tights and nothing else. He had seemed strangely agitated, changing his seat several times and ending up with Potts and Ebbing-Smith as if he thought they were likely to provide protection.

'Er, no thanks,' Brother Cornelius muttered. He closed his eyes until Baba's cleavage was removed. 'You see,'

94

he went on earnestly to Ebbing-Smith, 'I happened to pick up this little transistor in the street. Now the strange, the awesome thing is that God himself is speaking directly—using the media, you might say—to tell us what is happening to this poor little planet earth of ours.'

He paused for breath, his eyes rolling wildly. Potts and Ebbing-Smith made a dive for the transistor, which the priest was holding with reverence. The unusual energy of their movements brought the other men running up to the table. The piano stopped and the Martini shaker was still.

'Oh dear,' cried Baba. 'What's the matter now?'

It seemed to her sometimes that no sooner did she get what she wanted than it was taken away from her.

'Let me have that!' An ex-rugger blue grabbed the transistor. He held it high above his head, arm muscles rippling, and the other men stood round him in a circle.

At first there was silence. Brother Cornelius assumed an attitude of prayer. Then a voice—the woman's voice that had so alarmed them on the roof—began:

Sisters!
I speak to you of the Other Side.
None of the troubles of the old life are to be found
    there.
Harmony, peace and pleasure will be ours.
The goddess will be restored to her throne.
Rise! And fly across the exhausted waters at my side.

Unthinkingly, everyone turned to Brother Cornelius for an explanation. He cleared his throat and assumed an important expression. 'Brothers.' he began.

'But it didn't say brothers,' Ebbing-Smith cried in

exasperation. 'It said sisters. What is the meaning of all this, for God's sake?'

'It is God who knows,' Brother Cornelius stalled.

'Exhausted waters,' ruminated Potts. He had been clever at school but had always done what he could to hide the fact. 'It sounds to me as if something's going on on the other side of the river.' 'Battersea?' the rugger blue said truculently. 'What could be going on there?'

Baba, pushing her way through the pin stripes and sharkskin, piped up eagerly. 'It's all to do with a witch called Medea Smith,' she said. 'She's trying to get everyone to cross over there and have a new life. But don't go—I mean—'

Baba went unheard, she and Brother Cornelius being pushed to one side as the men shook the transistor violently for further news.

'Sisters!'—the voice came shrill and frightened this time—'Come to my aid! The wicked prince is overcoming us with his armies!'

The strongest of the Playboy patrons stood back at the wild crackling that emanated from the transistor. Pale, their minds racing and school memories re-activated as never before, they stared at each other in wild surmise.

Brother Cornelius dropped to his knees. Instinctively, Baba edged away, her tail guiding her to the exit and to safety.

The sounds of warfare and killing from the transistor grew until the doomed bar seemed no more than a vibrating hell, a black hole of exploding noise.

Then another sound—the now familiar sound of ripping, splitting, tearing masonry—overlaid the vindictive battle of the sexes on the transistor. The ether trembled at the decibel-force, and Baba could have sworn that red waves, like a dancing tide of lava, lapped the shadowy walls of the bar.

A great crack ran the length of the red plush carpeting. At first no more than an incision of scalpel fineness, it widened with hideous ease, swallowing in one gulp a handful of low tables and soft chairs, and darted to the bar, which split helplessly at its advance. The barman, shaker in hand, fell like a statuette into the void where a moment before his feet had stood.

The group of men, horror imprinted on their immobile faces, went down rigidly. A school photograph, the first and second eleven, they toppled sideways in a cardboard pose of death and vanished forever from Baba's life.

She gave a soft scream. Only Brother Cornelius remained, on his knees, praying by the edge of the crack. His lips moved silently—and in a horrifying parody of his prayer the lips of the crack moved too, glancing in a smile of derision at the toppling piano, yawning in an Amen of disaster as it stretched wide to include him. Baba, pushed against the far wall, found herself falling too—but away from the crack, down the bowed staircase of the Playboy, out into the street.

And the street was no more than the side of a steep hill now.

The pets had disappeared, buried under the new Lake District of Hyde Park and Park Lane. The remains of the funfair were entirely submerged.

Baba had no idea where she was going. She rolled fast, so fast she was hardly conscious of the pain from the jagged tube trains, the nips and nudges from broken sewage pipes, the new and ingenious torture instruments thrown up by the Crack. All she wanted was to die—and to die now.

Life without the Playboy could hardly be considered worth living. Medea Smith had tried to lead her to a nunnery on the other side. Pierre Courvoisier had tempted her with love, and had nearly drawn her to her death. A disgusting old man from a crooked house in Cheyne Walk had made obscene gestures to her as she ran in a headlong escape from her metallic enemy. She had been threatened by rape, vicious divorce proceedings and the jaws of angry dogs on her way to the only haven she knew was secure.

And now it was gone. Ebbing-Smith's bald head would never again nod foolishly as Potts explained the latest financial crisis. Visiting Americans would no longer stroll on fine evenings along the most exciting street in the world to London's most delightful meeting-spot. Two thousand years of civilization had led to the Playboy, and now it was buried, the bodies of Brother Cornelius and the young–old playboys of the Western World lying in serried ranks beneath the ruins.

16

Baba Rolls from Heaven to Hell, and Meets the Great Brain

If Baba could have wept, she would have let herself go completely. But she was rolling at too great a speed—and to her surprise she found her grief decreasing as she went, as if the inability to cry detracted somehow from the sorrow. Instead, something was stirring in Baba's mind—she found she thought less and less of the tinkling piano in the bar, the Marlene Dietrich number, the pleasure of carrying frosted drinks to unappreciative men—and more and more of the future.

After all, why should she give up now?

The first thing was to find some other people. And—yes—to find out why the Crack had happened, and what was likely to happen next. It was a new feeling, and Baba couldn't put a name to it. But as she rolled her excitement grew. She just couldn't wait to see what happened to her next.

With a bump, she came to rest against a great protuberance in the ground and scrambled to her feet.

'I think it's curiosity,' she said aloud as she examined the new feeling. 'And where am I now, I wonder?'

The protuberance, like the cranium of some giant intellect, was round and bald and shining. Baba walked round it carefully.

A faint buzzing noise came from inside. Baba frowned. A beehive? Not quite. There was definitely something in there though. And no way in. This was a puzzle she hadn't expected, and she leant against the dome to think. Then it all became clear to her. There were people in there—walled up alive!

The buzzing grew louder, and was accompanied by a feeble tapping noise. Like trying to break a stone with a feather, Baba thought sadly. How could it be possible to penetrate something so perfectly constructed, so obdurate, so impregnable? Perhaps this was the last attempt on the part of the prisoners to free themselves, for after a moment or so the noise stopped.

The silence that followed was dense and final, emphasized by a tricky little breeze which pulled at Baba's ears and sent scraps of week-old newspaper floating through the air. For the first time since the disaster Baba felt resignation rather than indignation or fear. So this was the end of the world: this was what it looked like. Sighing, she strolled to the summit of a small hill created by a No Entry sign and perched herself on a ledge made up out of sharp desk-tops and broken office furniture. A mound of flattened swivel chairs, already sprouting a thin moss, made a comfortable hummock, and Baba spread herself carefully on the fungoid upholstery before looking out over the ruins of London.

To the north, on the lower slopes of the great Hampstead range, the air was blue-grey from the small fires that had kindled themselves in the remains of stripped-pine kitchens. The south was flat and dead and still—even the seagulls had disappeared. Baba thought of Robinson Crusoe, and tears sprang to her eyes. She had always so much preferred the Swiss Family Robinson.

Only one thing moved. Baba watched it. With the same mixture of curiosity and resignation her eyes followed the quick, uncaring dance of the Crack as it ran like an adder in and out of the deserted streets. Sometimes it seemed to run towards her—then darted back, as if playing a mysterious version of Grandmother's Footsteps. It ran sideways, parting houses which fell groaning without each other's support. And up and down pavements—like an electric sewing machine, Baba thought, that undid stitches, tearing the material apart instead of hemming it together. With rapid pencil strokes it destroyed a hillock here, an area of parkland there. Trees fell, only to be thrown up, roots trembling violently skywards, in distant housing estates. Glass skyscrapers, their transparent stomachs filled for a moment with foliage and snapping twigs, nose-dived at the first insinuating approach of the Crack.

Baba's perch rocked but held firm. At the base, the Crack paused—then went, with a horrible decisiveness, it seemed to Baba, straight to the half-buried dome.

Baba scrambled to her feet. The dome split with a sound that was like a human cough.

From her insecure vantage point Baba peered in at its secrets. The split, she reflected with a wry smile, was like a parting cruelly drawn on a hairless head—but the teeth of the comb had sunk into the cranium itself and cut a line through the living matter of the brain.

What she saw made her draw back in disbelief. Deep down in the great skull, and gleaming like rows of sugar Easter eggs, were at least one hundred miniature crania, each one of them bald and slightly pointed. With a surge of panic Baba glanced at her own body. Had she grown suddenly to giant size, capable of taking up in one fistful all these tiny heads and rolling them like marbles in her palm? They were scholars: she could see the stacked shelves of books the height and width of postage stamps, the doll's house desks; was it possible that she, Baba, could crush all the great intellects of her time with one movement of finger and thumb, or assimilate, if she so chose, all the wisdom of the world with one sweeping gesture? Surely not, she thought miserably as she gazed down at them. Surely learning, for which she had always felt respect and reverence, was bigger and more awe-inspiring than this!

With the split in the roof the buzzing broke out anew.

A thin voice floated upwards. 'Silence in the Reading Room. There will be penalties for further talking!'

Baba pressed her eye to the crack in the surface of the dome. Despite her respect for scholarship she found it impossible to repress a smile. The bald heads were rushing about the great room, obviously in a state of agitation. With a minuscule hammer order was finally restored. The buzzing died down and the heads gathered together again to listen to the wielder of the hammer—a head that was broader, more purple-veined than the rest.

'There is no doubt', began a voice that was as clear and distant as a snapping icicle, 'that the present rift in south-east England is due to the southward movement of ice floes. I propose therefore—'

But at this a hubbub broke out. Feeble cries and the sound of fists banged on desks wafted up to the ceiling.

'Let Ebbing-Smith speak,' a voice sounded through a microscopic megaphone. 'He's the expert.'

I wonder if he's any relation, Baba thought wistfully as she remembered her old Playmate. But, try as she might, the tiny speck of pomposity was too far below for her to be able to detect a family resemblance.

Ebbing-Smith, who was in fact the father of the recently deceased playboy, having supported him for the past ten years on Nobel Prize money and now exhausted both financially and physically by the experience, rose with difficulty to his feet. Before speaking he glanced upwards once, his horn-rims catching the reflection of Baba's deep blue iris—then, terrified by what he had seen, he caught hold of the podium with both hands and began his speech.

'Ladies and Gentlemen.' With a courteous bow the old Professor beamed his recognition at the distinguished lady historians, all of them engaged on biographies of past Queens. 'I would like to put forward the theory, and substantiate it, need I add, that only the most extraordinary combination of climatic circumstances could have brought this disaster about.'

He paused for dramatic effect. It seemed to Baba that some of the reverence she had hoped for could be felt in the chamber; but at the same time she had to admit that a very faint tapping, like the sound of an army of termites, could be heard far beneath. It was probably silly to be disappointed, she tried to console herself, but surely the other scholars could listen to Ebbing-Smith with some show of manners?

'Increased pollution,' Ebbing-Smith quavered. 'Combined with the devilish machinations of the Americans.'

A faint halloo went up, accompanied by louder tapping from rows of identical yellow pencils, no more than wisps of straw to Baba's straining eye. Ebbing-Smith went on unperturbed.

'In order to bring on the monsoon season in Vietnam. The combined pressure on the atmosphere has caused a depression on the earth—and, unable to sustain the volume, the earth has split in two at the conjunction of the Gulf Stream and the higher channel ... '

The pencil tapping turned to desk-banging again and Ebbing-Smith's cranium sank defeated.

That sounds a likely explanation to me, Baba thought with excitement. Whyever can't the others listen to what he's saying?

A small skull, browner than the others and more sharply pointed, rose to the podium. There was a moment's expectant silence, followed by groans.

'What about Copernicus?' the parchment cranium shouted. 'Has it occurred to any one of us here—'

'Simple,' came a roar from a distant desk. 'You can forget about Copernicus and remember the Ruhr Valley. Brought by south-westerly winds the nuclear poisons of the over-industrialized zones—'

'I think', came the high, reproving voice of a lady scholar, 'that we should all stop here for a moment and remember the Manicheans. We must, brothers and sisters in adversity, bear in mind the children of darkness. Temporarily, they have overcome us. Evil reigns in the world. The Almighty has sent this warning.'

The lady scholar's head, curling fronds of grey hair in strange contrast to the baldness all around her, was pulled down forcibly by its neighbours.

Baba heaved a sigh and stepped back from the busy dome. She was inclined to favour the explanation of her lost lover's father—but one glance at the sky showed that neither pollution nor American-induced rain was in evidence.

The sky was a pale thrush-egg blue, with here and there a cumulus cloud that looked as if it had been painted on by a light-hearted Tintoretto. The faint sepia tinge of the last few days had vanished completely and there was hardly a hint of moisture in the air.

The sun, with a benign April radiance, sparkled over the new and curious landscape. Disappointed, but still hopeful, Baba set off in search of other explanations and friends.

17

How the Women were Overcome and the Work Force Lost

The battle had ended. Bowlby was going to be the only one to get to the other side now.

A palisade of jagged pieces of driftwood and rusted barbed wire from the river-bed surrounded the women's headquarters at World's End. In under an hour, with Thirsk's children as his work force, Bowlby had created an instant concentration camp. Abandoned Securicor Alsatians, found wandering hungrily at the doors of their old home in the Royal Hospital Road, guarded the encampment.

The wailing and fighting that had so terrified the doomed playboys on the transistor was reduced now to the occasional whimper. The women, exhausted and defeated by the onslaught, worked busily nonetheless in the derelict building. Bowlby had made it plain to them that he expected comfortable quarters, a safe home for his strangely child-like workers. Before evening mattresses must be made up from old rags passed in over the barbed wire by his wife (who smiled sometimes bountifully at the toiling women and offered jasmine tea from the kitchen of Courvoisier's house). Before night fell the improvised canteen must function perfectly, and the tins of baked beans unearthed on the shore opened and heated ready for consumption.

All contact with Medea Smith had ceased. It was as if the dream of a new life had never been. From time to time one of the women peered through a gap in the palisade at the great stretch of mud, dried now and split into crazily shaped pieces like the components of a giant jigsaw—at the chasm, which grew every hour wider and from which a faint, sulphurous smoke rose in languid puffs—and then turned back, sighing, to the work in hand.

Medea had arranged everything so beautifully.

A great steel rope, as strong and shining as a strand of the prophetess's hair, had been flung from the opposite bank to land only a few feet from the ruined church. It was dark, and the translucent snake had been spotted only by old Mrs Brown, whose arthritis kept her awake despite the promises of a glowing future on the other side.

When she had woken the other women and they had scrambled down to the metallic beach it was already too late. There was just time to see the cable-car, with lovely leopard-skin seats, to hear the beginning of Medea Smith's instructions—and then Bowlby and his army had been upon them and had overcome them. As they fought, each woman fighting for her life, the battle had inevitably edged in the direction of the cable-car.

There had been no time to secure the rope to the embankment and embark. Bowlby's forces fought savagely, insanely.

And the lovely coach, with seating capacity for at least fifty women, had exploded like a pantomime pumpkin as the battle surged around and in and out of it.

Now they were prisoners: wives and mothers of Thirsk's ex-patients. For all they knew, Medea Smith could be dead, blown to pieces at the other end of the cable as their coach exploded. And yet, from what they could see of the other side on this wickedly fine, calm morning, everything was going on exactly as before.

The same elegant cars drove with the same polite attention to the needs of fellow drivers.

New buildings were going up, exquisitely shaped as great birds, their glassy wings and capacious rounded bodies completed within hours.

Battersea Power Station had been carefully demolished and a complicated multi-level structure dedicated to pleasure was in the course of being erected.

At the topmost level a blue lake in the shape of a five-petalled flower glinted in the morning sun. Tiny boats, their sails like butterflies' wings danced about on the expanse of untroubled water. Below were arcades where people could be seen wandering contentedly—shops, probably, and twenty-four-hour outdoor film shows. And still lower, what seemed to be a replica of Paris's Left Bank, with a painted strip of river and microscopic bereted men selling books and water colours beside it.

At ground level, a row of fountains splashed ruby-coloured liquid into bright mosaic basins. The lucky inhabitants, as they passed, held out gold and silver goblets to catch the sparkling wine.

Even Bowlby was impressed. He paced up and down beside his bridge, his impatience growing as the clumsy labourers fumbled with the makeshift girders. In the last ten minutes, over where Southwark had been, the beginnings of the greatest office block ever were under way. Shaped like a cigar five hundred feet high, the first block had gone up the previous evening; and Bowlby stared with envy at the bands of stained glass windows, the word Enterprise that glittered from the top in letters as high as a cathedral spire.

'What d'you think it says the other side?' he asked McDougall, who was standing beside him. 'Free? Free Enterprise?'

'Perhaps,' McDougall answered with a smile. Since Bowlby's bridge had got under way he had adopted a tired, shrugging manner, as if it mattered little to him whether he got to the other side or not.

'Just look at them,' Bowlby fumed. He pointed a shaking finger at his workers. 'We'll never get there at this rate.'

It was true that Thirsk's children showed little intelligence when it came to building bridges. Ned and Mary, who had once been given a Meccano set by a friendly social worker, liked to pull down the girders once they had been set up. Mrs Withers, a sufferer from vertigo even before regression, clung to each section of the bridge as it was levered into position and had to be prised off before work could continue.

'That's what's wrong with this country,' Bowlby went on. 'What on earth kind of system have they got over there? I mean, look at the speed they build at. By the time we get there it's not going to be easy to run industry. In fact, if they've been watching our methods they'll probably laugh us to scorn when we arrive. He sighed, gazing anxiously at the precarious bridge as it slowly and shakily approached the Crack it-self.

It was McDougall who saw the dangers ahead and barked orders to drop tools. Sweat pouring off their brows, Thirsk's children collapsed gratefully on the concrete-hard mud.

'They haven't noticed the Crack,' he pointed out. And, much to Bowlby's annoyance, laughed.

'They were just going to carry on building in the void,' he went on, still laughing. 'You must admit, Max, we haven't got much of a chance of getting there in one piece. I ask you, shouldn't we consider at this point ...'

'Giving up?' Bowlby's eyes widened in horror. He strode across the jumbled scrap-heap of the river-bed and took up a thoughtful attitude by the edge of the chasm. 'It's all a question of suspension,' he shouted back at the sceptical McDougall.

'We won't go on without more sweeties,' the workers chorused when they saw Bowlby.

'We want our Daddy,' Ned added in a savage tone.

McDougall, still recovering from his laughing fit, coughed vigorously into his handkerchief.

'Time for a break,' he called to the industralist. 'Send them over to the women for elevenses.'

Bowlby shook his head impatiently. There, across the gulf, lay the dream of his lifetime: perfectly synchronized workers putting up monuments of incomparable beauty to the endurance of progress and capital. There, only fifty yards or so from his eyes lay the proof of the via-bility of free enterprise, the satisfactions to be gained from hard work and suitable emolument. This was hardly the time to retreat defeated to the barbarity that lay behind him.

'You see this hole?' he asked the children carefully. At the same time, he raised his megaphone, constructed from the last-ever copy of the *Daily Telegraph*, to his lips. If need be, the final provisions must be brought out: the Chartreuse found deep in the cellars of Courvoisier's house, and the Dom Perignon he had reserved for his triumphal arrival at the other side.

'More sweeties,' screamed Mrs Withers.

'I don't like the hole,' remarked poor Jo-Jo, who was staring down compulsively at the void.

Bowlby shouted for his wife. As he did so, the sweet sadness he had known for several days now made a constriction in his throat and spread, with a treacly uncertainty, to his bowels. If only that delectable mud-covered girl, the girl who haunted his dreams nightly, who had run into his life and disappeared from it in the direction of the alien hinterland, could be here with him now to hold his hand and share his coming victory! He had thought for one glorious moment, as he battled with the women on the shore, so reminiscent of Dunkirk with its broken concrete slabs and barbed wire, that one of the girls he found struggling in his arms was none other than the lovely, fleeing nymph. But no—adorable though she was (and for some reason wearing a pair of fluffy ears that tickled his chin as he overpowered her)—this girl said she had never run naked along Cheyne Walk. Her name was Noreen. She was pretty, and had smiled seductively at her conqueror. But, try as he might, he was incapable of falling in love with her instead. The best thing was to bear in mind that everyone in the end would cross the bridge and enter Bowlby's empire. And why not the girl he had so fleetingly glimpsed? Bowlby here was powerless, even a figure of fun. Bowlby on the other side —

All the same, it was with a feeling of impending loss that he called on his wife to bring the emergency provisions. Once they had crossed the Crack and he had assumed his position of power, would it ever be possible to cross back again and find her? Gritting his teeth, Bowlby boomed for the champagne and chartreuse.

Lady Bowlby's answer was so faint that only McDougall, still on shore, could hear it. Once more he doubled up with laughter; Bowlby, frowning, marched towards him. It was interesting, he reflected, how a situation like this showed a man for what he was. Some inner decadence and corruption caused McDougall, at the last minute, to give up hope. And precisely the same situation gave Bowlby courage and determination on an unprecedented scale.

'The supplies are finished,' McDougall giggled when Bowlby reached him. 'Your dear wife gave them all to the women this morning.'

Before Bowlby could explode with rage, a series of piercing screams went off behind him at the edge of the Crack. He ran back, swearing loudly at the undisciplined behaviour of his workers. 'Once we're over there,' he muttered grimly as he arrived breathless at the scene of chaos. 'Then you'll see, my dear chaps!'

The children were peering down into the Crack and giving out cries of encouragement. Mrs Withers seized Bowlby's ankle, nearly bringing him down. Her eyes were gleaming with excitement.

'Daddy!' she burbled up at him. 'Daddy down there. Me going there too!'

As soft as the mist that rises from a lake at sunrise, a pall of fine smoke rose from the Crack. The children cheered happily. When it had cleared a little, Bowlby tiptoed nervously to the edge of the chasm and gazed down.

He could just make out, huddled together like men trapped in some Satanic mine, two black-robed figures, their faces as black as their gowns. One of the faces attached to the robed bodies was looking up at him—a tangled beard flecked with red dust waggled at the end of the grimy jaw.

'Negroes!' Bowlby cried out in alarm. It was with the greatest effort that he refrained from stepping back from the Crack and fleeing to shore.

Thirsk's eyes shone like coals. His voice, rising with the sulphurous fumes from the subterranean regions beneath the river-bed, was hoarse and terrifying. 'Where are my children?' he called.

Harcourt, shrill and piping, repeated the question. Bowlby's workers clustered more closely round the Crack. Shouts of delight rang out.

'Come to my tunnel,' Thirsk croaked. 'Deep in the womb of the earth—'

No more was needed. With the promise of the birth trauma ahead, the patients leapt happily down. It was clearly soft down there, for there were no cries of pain, only the thuds of their landing and the wet kisses bestowed by Thirsk on his lost children. Bowlby groaned in anguish.

'What about my bridge?' he screamed into the chasm.

Then a thought occurred to him. These strange black-robed creatures had probably already made a tunnel to the other side. McDougall could stay here, for all Bowlby cared. And his wife—he hoped he would never see her again. She could stay in the women's camp and starve to death if she wished. All he had to do was jump.

He paused for a moment, looking round him at the fine sunny morning and the untidy, unsuccessful bridge. What did he have to lose?

Bowlby landed on Thirsk's shoulders. The huge analyst placed him on the ground with a snort of contempt.

'And who are you?' he growled at him.

The two men glared at each other in the darkness of the roughly hewn tunnel. Behind them a portion of the river-bed sank slowly, coming to rest in the underground passage like the door of a Biblical tomb.

18

Baba Melts in the Heat of Revolutionary Ardour

The sun climbed high in the sky and sent a punishing golden heat down on to the contorted landscape below. Splinters of broken glass from windshields and blasted typing pools lay in the streets; and to Baba, dazed with fatigue and loss of sense of direction, the myriad rainbows they sent out made an unending prism of reflections of yellow and green and red.

The furry ears were hot and scratchy now, and Baba's tail made an uncomfortable weight between her legs. She walked, sometimes in circles, sometimes along motorways that rose grandly above humble dwelling-places and then stopped suddenly as if the designer had lost interest before they could reach their destination.

'I should have stayed with Medea Smith and the women,' Baba sighed to herself. 'They've probably crossed to the other side now—they're very likely having the most wonderful life.'

She pictured to herself, as she dragged her weary feet over the twisted tarmac, the domes of splendid dance halls on the other side, the sparkling open-air bars where food of every nationality was served.

'There'll be a Greek taverna,' Baba murmured. 'And bierkellers where delicious cold beer is brought the instant you ask for it. And then I might dress up myself and go to the biggest hotel as a hostess. I wonder what that would be like?'

As Baba mused, pausing often to rub her back or sit disconsolately on an overturned island, the sun grew hotter and the picture of the big hotel cooler and more delightful.

'Fountains in the hall,' said poor Baba aloud. 'And a great underground swimming-pool with dark green plastic water-lily leaves floating on it. And on each leaf a frosted cocktail—yes (for she was getting hungry too) an avocado pear in a bed of ice and a White Lady beside it with a lovely little cherry sticking out the top ... '

Baba's left foot struck something hard and cold, and she gave a cry of pain.

Looking up, she thought for a moment that the sun had gone in at last and a great grey cloud had taken its place. A blessed coolness, even a slight dampness filled the air.

Then she screamed again. A horrible little man was crouching just above her head. All round him, as far as the eye could see, was an expanse of grim, wet stone broken by ledges that supported other monsters just as terrifying. Decayed grey teeth snarled down in grimaces of hostility. Listless eyes outstared her as she gazed pathetically up at them for a sign of friendship. Here the sun was unable to penetrate. Here the Crack had darted in vain, leaving only faint fissures in the massive walls.

'Where can I be?' moaned Baba. 'How do I get round this one?'

At least it was cool in the shadow of the vast mausoleum. Baba pressed her aching shoulders against the walls, feeling with a shudder of relief the deathly touch of stone on flesh. Even the sight of a beetle crawling carelessly from one lichen-filled crack to another failed to move her away.

Something hard and sticky dropped on to Baba's head.

Too afraid to cry out again, she leapt back and stared upwards. The little grinning devil was melting! His leer, directed, it seemed, straight at Baba, assumed ridiculous proportions. A gnarled hand, fingers arranged in some ancient imprecation, plopped to the ground beside Baba's feet. To right and left, swaying and cracking on their ledges, the other demons began to do the same.

The sun was winning the battle. From the highest buttress—so high that Baba had to fling her head right back to see where it soared to meet the sky—lead cannonballs turned to black treacle and poured over the sides to splash beside her on the ground. With a deep groan that sounded like the breaking of bones, the great wall settled down several feet into its foundations.

'I'd better get away from here,' Baba told herself. 'This is getting dangerous!'

The sound of voices paralysed her just as she was about to turn and run for her life.

They weren't friendly voices, either: some were shrill and querulous, and seemed to be demanding some sort of human sacrifice. Others were deep and menacing, theatening to put an end there and then to the shrill ones if they didn't hold their tongues at once.

Baba dug her carmine fingernails deep into a crack in the wall and pulled herself up six feet. She was grateful now for the athletic body which had brought her such speedy promotion at the Playboy. Another agile leap and she found herself on the ledge where the melting devil had stood. She was on a level now with the other grotesque creatures—and she could feel the reason for their impending disintegration. The sun beat on her head like a stone hammer. Her nose and lips flattened into a gargoyle grin. Heart beating, she turned to face the crowd, her bare toes gripping the ledge and her arms spreadeagled against the wall.

'What I say is,' shrieked one of the shrill voices below, 'let's find him now and string him up! Beat him to death! Crucify him!'

From her perch Baba could see that the crowd was divided into two elements.

There were the scholars from the Reading Room—they had clambered out, she supposed, when the last preposterous explanation for the Crack had been delivered —and there was a motley group of middle-aged people in rags. It was impossible to tell who they were, but it was clear from their fresh indignation that they hadn't been in London at the time of the cataclysm. 'Calm, calm,' Ebbing-Smith Senior was saying. 'We have no reasonable proof that the causes for the disaster proffered by our Birmingham and Manchester friends here are in any way correct.'

'Better than your hypothesis,' snapped one of the lady historians.

'Listen here.' A portly, ragged man (a Birmingham businessman, Baba supposed) stepped out of the crowd and waved his arms for silence. 'I don't care what you eggheads have worked out in your museum,' he went on when everyone was looking at him obediently. 'All I know is that we've had to walk all the way South and now you won't listen to what really happened. Theories are nothing to facts is what I say—'

A hubbub broke out from the scholars at this and Baba found herself wriggling with impatience so that she almost fell from her precarious ledge. If only they would let him say what really did happen, she thought, and felt tears of despair sting her eyes. What's the matter with them?

A young scholar, prematurely bald and wearing horn-rim glasses cracked by the heat of the walk from the Reading Room, was making a show of admiring the building rather than listen to the expert from Birmingham.

He strolled around the base of the great wall, his murmurs of appreciation drifting up to poor Baba's agonizing resting-place.

'I must say that the Abbey shows us even today that the methods of construction used in the Middle Ages were infinitely superior to ours,' he remarked to one of the younger lady historians. 'Our Abbey has resisted every onslaught, don't you feel?'

'I know where everyone has gone,' insisted the Birmingham businessman. 'And I know who the culprit is.'

The right arm and devil's fork of a large and fast-melting triton fell to the ground, narrowly missing the young scholar. He looked up apprehensively.

'Watch it!' cried the shrill Northern faction of the crowd. 'The bloody place is collapsing!'

All eyes gazed upwards, and trained themselves on Baba. She held her breath, turned to stone herself as the ravening faces peered up at her. 'That's an interesting one.'

The young scholar pointed her out. 'A female gargoyle in the early fourteenth-century tradition. Demonstrating the evil of woman, the misogyny of the time. How strange to contemplate the feelings of the anonymous stone-mason as he chipped away at the image of what he most dreaded and desired! How moving to—'

But at this point the crowd from the North bore down on the young scholar and silenced him. Slowly, painfully, Baba's heartbeats returned to normal.

When the uproar died down, Ebbing-Smith could be heard once more. 'I suggest', he said in the reasonable tone which had led so many to be fooled by his unlikely theories in the past, 'that we go to the river and confront this speculator McDougall with the matter. If our friends here are telling the truth, he will be unable to deny the consequences of his actions.' 'McDougall suggested to me', the businessman went on obstinately, 'a deal whereby I supplied the materials for a bloody great dormitory town on the other side of the river and supplied them at half price in return for what he termed "residential advantages" this side.'

'Disgusting,' muttered a Hungarian scientist from amongst the dense group of scholars.

'And I maintain,' spoke up a man from amongst the group of itinerant merchants, 'I maintain he put too many people over there too quickly. Hence the land to the south of the river became over-weighted and these cracks appeared in the surface of the earth.'

'Most unscientific,' sighed an attractive young geologist on whom Baba looked down longingly. 'We can but go and see, I suppose.'

The crowd, muttering discontentedly, turned away

from the frowning façade of the Abbey and went off down a narrow street Baba had never seen before.

So that's where the river lies, she thought to herself in excitement. If I follow them I'll find Medea and she'll take care of me. Thank God for that!

Even as she sprang down from the ledge and ran happily after the vengeful crowd, Baba felt the stirrings of an impossible hunger.

And as she caught up with the straggling Birmingham and Manchester wives in the tail of the procession she realized they were feeling the same thing.

'If I don't have a pasty and a nice cup of tea I'm not going any further,' a kindly looking woman remarked fiercely. 'How about you, Mabel?'

'I'll go on strike without,' Mabel agreed.

The presence of foreigners in her city had suddenly made Baba realize where she was. After their first surprise at seeing her amongst them, the women agreed to be led to the best food shop in the world. It was with some difficulty that Baba located the handsome geologist; but once found, he admitted to an appetite that would brook no refusal.

'I daresay it's worth the detour,' he said loftily as Baba tugged at his arm.

Without anyone noticing them, the hungry group broke off from the crowd and followed Baba to Knightsbridge.

19

A Sailor to the Rescue

The sails of the *Lady Merrie Englande* flapped listlessly as she tacked home on the last leg of her round-the-world-journey.

Walter Rugglesby was in his cabin writing up the log. A knighthood awaited him at Plymouth, but he had decided to surprise the world press and TV by sailing up the Thames instead and disembarking at the Tower of London. 'Rugglesby the Difficult Genius' was the term used to describe him in American and British Sunday papers—for Rugglesby had demanded a doubling of the prize money, and 'a wife in every port', which meant that a pretty girl in national costume in each port passed by Rugglesby had had to be paid to wave vigorously at him as he went by. And that was not all. Rugglesby had offended good taste by designing his own coat of arms before the world trip, instead of waiting for the Queen to confer a knighthood on him. In anticipation of the vast prize money, he had built a glass and aluminium house with 364 rooms, explaining in his interviews that he only intended to leave home on one day a year, and would spend the others each in a different setting—and when asked, with some suspicion, on which day he planned to go out had replied Christmas Day, to go and visit his mother. It was thus that Rugglesby continued to entrance and intrigue his public.

The *Lady Merrie Englande* was no ordinary boat either. She appeared, when sailing on the high seas, to be no more than a catamaran — but Rugglesby had so planned and built her that she could cope with dry land too, skimming like a hovercraft when she chose and growling into four-wheel-drive like a Land-Rover when the terrain was tough. Rugglesby's next trip, in fact, would consist of crossing the Sahara in her; and the one after was scheduled to be the ascent of Everest; but he had mentioned none of this to the media. His landing at the Tower and subsequent gliding through the streets of London to the Savoy was a secret which he shared only with his tame albatross and the monotonous, heaving waves in which he had lived and slept for a whole year past.

'I am God,' Rugglesby wrote in the log. 'Between me and humanity are nine hierarchical bands. A fine day today, wind slight N.E. Albatross finished my home-made plum cake at 11.43 BST. Sighted the white cliffs at 08.56.'

With a sigh of satisfaction he closed the great book, due to be auctioned at Sotheby's later in the year, and went up on deck.

The shores of England were nearer than he had expected. Or rather, they seemed to have come out to meet him. Beaches ten miles long and oddly dry stretched to the mouth of the Thames, as if the tides had ceased to function and the land under the sea had been left exposed for several days.

Dried seaweed made a ragged carpet over the cracked mud. Dead fish and half-opened shells lay like the remains of a huge maritime banquet, and overhead seabirds flapped and dived like vultures.

Rugglesby went to the controls. He felt no surprise at the change from sea to landscape, but was slightly alarmed at the absence of a welcoming committee and eager crowd. He had been almost sure that his surprise arrival had been guessed at, and that only the naive would go to Plymouth in the expectation of finding him there.

The *Lady Merrie Englande* skimmed over the unnatural shore to the mouth of the Thames, and then paused. Rugglesby rubbed at his eyes in amazement. The Thames was as wide as the Amazon. A great crack at least fifty feet wide lay along its centre like a giant cobra.

With a flicker of panic, Rugglesby consulted his maps. Was it possible that he had arrived in South America by mistake, that the trusty *Lady Merrie* had been going round in circles for the last three months?

Then he remembered who he was. If he said this was England, then it was England. True, he had lost contact in the last few days with his sponsors. He had imagined that their excitement at his return was too great to be expressed—and that they had been busy preparing the Savoy for his welcome party. Now he saw that other things had occupied their imaginations.

Gritting his teeth in annoyance Rugglesby put the *Lady Merrie* into low fly. Gracefully the lovely amphibian glided up the Crack towards her destination.

The women in Bowlby's internment camp saw the *Lady Merrie* and let out a great cry of hope and anguish.

Lady Bowlby's supplies of champagne and chartreuse from Pierre Courvoisier's cellars had dried up the day before, and although Lady Bowlby herself had joined them on the strength of her gesture she was no longer popular there. Old Mrs Brown stirred up trouble in the camp. 'It's all her fault. She's the one who ought to go, in my opinion.'

'We should draw lots,' insisted the gentle Noreen. 'It wouldn't be fair otherwise.'

The question in hand at the time was who should be eaten and the best way to arrive at the decision. Hunger had reached terrible proportions—and the obvious victims, the heiress and her small husband who could still be seen prone in deckchairs on the perpendicular lawns of Courvoisier's house, were protected by Lady Bowlby.

'You just can't do it,' she kept saying at the meetings of the Food Committee. 'She's such a sweet girl. And she was so lucky to find him.'

Lady Bowlby's fate was on the point of being decided when the *Lady Merrie* was seen streaming up the river-bed like an unwieldy bird with canvas wings. The women ran to the edge of the camp and climbed up the palisades, barbed wire tearing at their legs and skirts.

Noreen climbed highest, her golden hair caught by the light breeze and fanning out behind her so that she resembled, to Rugglesby's starved eyes, a mermaid on a pole in a sea of rubble and broken concrete slabs.

'Ahoy!' Noreen cried. 'Ahoy there!'

Her musical voice brought the flying-boat down on the dried river-bed, only a few feet from the Crack. Rugglesby got out and walked smiling up to the vision. So this was the Welcome Committee! He might have guessed they would think of something unusual in the way of greeting. And all women! He frowned slightly at this, and frowned more when he saw the ugly, ravening faces of the women behind the stockade. Only Noreen was beautiful. What was the meaning of this?

'Who are you?' cooed Noreen. Never had she felt more in need of Baba's friendship and support than now, for all their futures depended on how she played it. And Baba had been so much more experienced at the Playboy.

Rugglesby gasped at the question. Then he burst out laughing. Sycophantically, all the women laughed too.

'I think you know the answer to that,' he parried. 'Come here, wench.'

'If you have a knife,' said Noreen, pointing helplessly down at the wire. 'You could let us out, you know.'

Rugglesby was enjoying himself thoroughly by now.

'And would I be without a knife?' he chuckled. 'Here, ladies.'

The wire was cut; with some dignity Lady Bowlby came forward and introduced herself. Rugglesby was slightly puzzled—it was an odd committee, but there was a Lady on it so it must be all right. And when Noreen asked in her sweet way if they could all go aboard the *Lady Merrie* and make a trip to the other side, he consented with a shrug.

'What's been going on here then?' he asked as they sailed effortlessly over the Crack and landed on the far bank. 'I mean, everything round where you were seems to have fallen down. Been a Revolution or something?'

There was nothing Rugglesby dreaded more than a Revolution, as it detracted from his personal publicity.

'Everything's fine this side,' Noreen said breathlessly as she stepped out of the *Lady Merrie*. There, hair shining like a candelabra of electrified glass, arms held out like the Lord Jesus welcoming his flock, stood Medea Smith.

It was too good to be true. Unimaginable. They had arrived at the Other Side!

'Certainly been some changes since I set out a year ago,' Rugglesby remarked in a disapproving tone. He turned to Lady Bowlby for information. 'This what they've done to Battersea Funfair?' he asked.

Even Lady Bowlby was incapable of answering him. As if drawn by some great, invisible magnet the women walked up the carpeted ramp and surrounded Medea. As they stood all together embracing, their ragged clothes and gaunt features contrasting strangely with the contented faces of the passing inhabitants and occupants of the big, shark-shaped cars that drove quietly along the ribbons of the multi-level cities-within-cities, Rugglesby was reminded of a painting of a band of pilgrims he had once seen.

Scratching his head, he looked right and left and up and down.

Silently, the women melted away and were swallowed up by the strolling crowd.

20

Baba Visits Harrods and Takes an Open-Air Dip

It was strange, Baba reflected, how showing foreigners round a place gave you a feeling of authority, a pleasant sense of control and well-being.

Even if you were hungry—so hungry that the ruins of houses had come to look like dishes of leftovers, the scraps of scattered furniture like burnt meat, the wrecked roads like crusts of hard dried bread. And she was thirsty too, so that every fragment of shattered glass lying in the street became an enticing pool of clear, cool water; but nevertheless she was determined to do her duty as a hostess and give as much pleasure to these poor women from Birmingham and Manchester as she possibly could.

Only the young geologist seemed disgruntled by the proceedings. 'So where's this wonderful food you promised us?' he complained as Baba brightly pointed out the site of the former St George's Hospital and, in the distance, the gaunt shell of Buckingham Palace.

'We're coming to it,' smiled Baba. Things weren't going as well with him as she had hoped, but the way to a man's heart, after all, was his stomach—and after he had eaten she hoped he would feel better-disposed towards her.

'Just think,' she went on, 'I had no idea where we were this morning. When I came to that funny big dome I had no idea what it was!'

'Did you anyway?' said the geologist, whose name, appropriately, was Stone, in a cross voice. 'Ever been to the British Museum in your life?'

'Oh, my feet are killing me,' moaned one of the trippers.

'I haven't read a book for ages,' Baba admitted, dimpling. 'The last one was *Black Beauty*. Don't you think it's lovely?'

Stone was silent, and they all walked on without further comment. Baba's group were now in the remains of a fine, winding boulevard; and it was clear from the expensively dressed dummies lying here and there on the upturned tarmac that it had once been a shopping area of the very highest quality.

When the formidable sandstone ruins of Harrods came into view a gasp of admiration went up.

'Petra in Knightsbridge,' bragged Stone. 'I wonder if it will be possible to hire a donkey to take us round the site.'

Baba, trembling with anticipation, led her guided tour to the portals of the fantastic monument. Here, she knew, she must explain the significance of the place to her visitors—must tell them, insisting in the face of their disbelief, that in the old days you could get anything here, even a funeral.

'Or an elephant, if you order in advance,' she sparkled at her guests. 'And on the ground floor we find the Food Hall—'

A wild stampede left her last words unheard. With their last reserves of energy the business wives ran into the dark temple to merchandise and fought their way through gloves and tights that hung like phantom cobwebs to the decorated inner vaults.

Some clawed at lobsters, others peeled quails' eggs with feverish speed and thrust them into their mouths like sweets. Whole sides of smoked salmon were roughly chopped with meat axes. In the confectionery department, where the glacé cherries on the little iced cakes gleamed like red eyes in the dusty gloom, the wives ran amok. Meringues, *milles*, *feuilles*, eclairs, rum babas were pulled from cracked glass shelves. Doughnuts went down in one gulp. Five-tiered wedding cakes swayed and fell, the minuscule bridal couple pirouetting one last time before being crunched in two by hasty teeth.

Baba and Stone remained in the Fish Hall. Stone was sawing at the haunches of a sucking pig, the main feature of the central display stand, and cramming the raw flesh into his mouth. From time to time he ran over to the great marble slabs of gaping cod, halibut and rainbow trout and picked out a handful of prawns—and each time he did so it seemed to Baba that the eyes of the young piglet stared at his retreating back with reproach. It was impossible, she knew: the eyes were no more than two shining black olives, with pimento eyebrows arched coyly above them; but it did seem such a shame to hack away at him like that.

Stone's cannibalistic approach in no way detracted from his attractiveness to Baba. And as he munched, swaying crazily by now from the *Boucherie* to the beautiful ornamental arrangement of kippers, as he ran, destroying everything in his path, literally eating his way through the place, she thought she saw the beginnings of love for her stir in his breast.

'Where's the drink kept?' he muttered thickly, bumping against her on one of his wild runs. 'For God's sake, woman, aren't you hungry?'

Baba didn't want to explain that in her opinion a girl eating too ravenously wasn't an enticing sight, so she smiled demurely at him and said nothing. It had been with the greatest difficulty that she had restrained herself from behaving like the other women: only a few sprigs of decor parsley and a quail's egg had gone down her delicate throat.

At Stone's bidding, Baba slipped away to the wine shop and returned with a bottle of gin and two bottles of hock. Scorning the gin, Stone broke open the neck of the hock bottle on a marble slab and drank greedily.

'Not too bad,' he remarked with satisfaction. 'Here, I think there's a little left. Have some.'

He passed her the bottle casually, but Baba could sense Stone's growing awareness of her ravishing body and sweet little ears. With a tail waggle that reminded her sadly of the past, she accepted the dregs of wine and sipped prettily. And when she was offered a chunk of raw pig on the end of a butcher's knife she let it slip down with apparent relish.

Sated with cakes and soft drinks, the business wives staggered back to the great hall in search of their guide.

'Time we got to the river,' one of them announced shrilly. 'Where's that courier gone?'

'Oh look!' cried another. 'Really! I must say!'

Stone and Baba lay entwined amongst the discarded lobster claws and half-eaten lamb chops on the floor of the Food Hall. Paper cutlet-frills crackled under their sinuously moving bodies. The backbone of a plucked chicken snapped under their weight as they kissed and rolled and finally came to orgasm. Panting, gasping with pleasure they pulled themselves to a sitting position to find a row of angry eyes fixed on them.

'Dear oh dear,' said Baba as she wiped the blood from a tray of calves liver from her new outfit. 'I suppose we'd better be going now.'

'I want to exit through Drugs and Perfumery,' snapped a tall middle-aged woman. 'Get a look at the bath essences.'

'Handbags! Stationery!' chorused the others.

With difficulty, Baba led her furious guests out of the emporium and on the road to Chelsea. Her back was aching and her clothes smelt of shellfish but she was happy.

As Stone, Baba and the wives were making their way to the banks of the river the businessmen and scholars were on the point of arriving there by another route. As always happened with new arrivals to the scene, a gasp of disbelief went up at the sight of the drained river-bed and the enormous Crack, which stretched now almost the whole width of the expanded Thames.

Disoriented at first, the ill-assorted company wandered down Cheyne Walk, oohing and aahing at the slumped houses and general appearance of disintegration.

It wasn't long before McDougall was spotted, however. Lying at an uncomfortable angle on his perilous lawn, he was in the process of being handed a cup of grass tea by the heiress and her husband.

'It's the best we can manage I'm afraid,' the husband

said sycophantically. McDougall had promised him a fifty-fifty share in the redevelopment of all London north of the river, and he eagerly awaited overcrowding to become unbearable on the other side.

'Thanks a lot,' McDougall said in his languid way. 'What the hell's that, coming towards us?'

So sure was McDougall by now of his empire that he felt convinced of his ability to handle the occasional group of leftover hippies. Yawning, he gazed up Cheyne Walk at the approaching mob.

'Visitors?' squeaked the husband.

Several of the scholars who had previously held liberal or even High Tory views were now left-wing, almost communist. Fuming with rage at the destruction of London, the disintegration of society and their lowly position in what remained of it, they pressed forward, jagged planks in hand. The businessmen, confused as to their own future but unchanged politically, followed them at a safe distance.

'Capitalist hyena!' Ebbing-Smith snorted. 'String him up! Imperialist lackey!'

McDougall shifted restlessly on the dry, sloping grass. He rose, tried to back away from the radical scholars, and slipped down the steep gradient into the street.

A cheer of derision went up from the angry men. Flushing, McDougall pulled himself up again.

'A lot to answer for,' Ebbing-Smith was saying as the tumult died down. 'How do you account for these events. Eh?'

'He was the man all right,' a businessman put in. 'Said he'd rehouse every single inhabitant of London this side of the river—put them in dormitories on the other side, he said.'

McDougall faced the mob, his calm disappearing visibly. There was an unpleasant lull as the men awaited their moment to lynch.

Baba's party came down the flat plains of Danvers Street and arrived in Cheyne Walk. Thrown off their guard by the appearance of their wives, the businessmen moved away uneasily. Ebbing-Smith barked an order for them to stop where they were, but it was too late. Taking advantage of the moment of chaos, McDougall had slipped away.

Then Baba pointed, her hand shaking with terror, in the direction of Chiswick and Kew. The scream she let out was so bloodcurdingly loud that everyone stood still, staring first at Baba's trembling fingers and then at the great curve of the river-bed. Ebbing-Smith gave a low moan and clutched the lady historian's sharp figure for support.

A huge tidal wave of water was bearing down on them. A twenty-foot wall, solid and implacable, it came at the speed of a monster in a nightmare—slowly, but too fast for anyone to have a chance to turn back before it was on them. The sound was a low roar, like the sound of jungles falling, flattened by a tornado. It was only half a mile away now and the crest was visible: it seemed to carry on its head a jumble of chairs and tables and broken driftwood of every description—and what looked to the sickened eyes of the spectators like legs and arms, thrashing feebly in the brown foam.

The Crack was filling up. Miraculously, the water chose only the river-bed for its thunderous arrival and as it swirled past them the little band sighed and sobbed with relief.

The Crack disappeared under the torrent. The water rose to within a foot of the embankment, found its level, and stopped. Bowlby's makeshift bridge was swept away.

Clasping each other with delight, Baba and Stone ran down to the river to wash.

21

Over the Crack and Far Away

A bearded man sat alone by the Serpentine in Hyde Park. Slowly, patiently, he was mending an antiquated balloon. While he did so he whistled through his teeth and smiled from time to time, reminding himself of the pleasures and excitements that lay ahead in the new world; and the fact that he alone, of all men, would be able to guide the human race through the snares and difficulties that lay ahead.

Waters had buried his wife and family some time ago. Their graves, crude memorials to a way of life that had no purpose or meaning, lay scattered in the patchy grass of the park. An up-ended bench marked one, a broken model boat another. He had made no effort to twist the improvised tombstones into the shape of the cross: something else was at the root of the Universe and he cared little now who knew he thought that.

'The Age of Aquarius,' Waters hummed to himself. 'Jeremy Waters, Superstar!'

The balloon was ready at last. And so, Waters reflected as he climbed aboard complacently, was its owner. Since the disappearance of Baba and the terrible heart-wrenching pain he had suffered then, he had become an entirely reconstructed man. *L'homme integrale*, as the

Cubans would have it. In future, Waters would live only for the public good. He would weep only for public causes. If men died in war, Waters would feel a limb amputated. There had been too much concern with private matters, too little for the tragic, sometimes ridiculous ways of humanity. When his family had died of starvation, Waters had had to admit to a sense of relief.

The balloon rose easily in the steady wind and drifted south to the river. The ruins of London had never looked more beautiful than now, the crescents of South Kensington no more than jaw formations in which teeth had once stood white and strong, the Natural History Museum as skeletal and forbidding as its prehistoric contents.

Waters lifted his binoculars and gazed through them as if quizzing a *demi-mondaine* at the opera.

There was the Kings Road, as deserted and forlorn as he had expected to find it. No more boutiques now for the philistine pop singers and their musk-scented, frizzle-haired girls!

There was Cheyne Walk, an enjoyable symbol of the end of capitalism. Rich mens' houses as helpless as abandoned toy accordions. Prize-winning gardens filled with crushed delphiniums and split lawns on which the grass would never grow again.

And there—Waters started, adjusted the sights and stared again—there was the river Thames, flowing eagerly and joyously between wide banks.

The river showed no signs of having dried up, of having ever in its majestic history lost its sense of importance, its knowledge of the role it played in the life of the English people. Brown, heavy water rolled ponderously under destroyed bridges. Seagulls sat snugly on the important current.

The wind rose, not playfully but with a strong pull which Waters was unable to counter. He was going too high now, and threw himself about in the balloon so as to keep low over the river. The balloon sank, and he found himself only twenty feet above the muddy swirl, gazing anxiously at the sky for further guidance.

Several people were crossing the river on rafts. Paddling madly with chairlegs and pieces of driftwood, they were almost submerged by water and were groaning loudly as they went.

Waters directed a godlike smile at them. How desperate and futile seemed the efforts of mankind in the face of perils like these! He pitied the motley raftloads of men and women, each one intent on his own salvation.

Then he saw Baba. She was lying back in the arms of a handsome young man and was as relaxed as if out on a punt on a summer's day. Her lovely face, ears lying back docilely against her head, was directed straight at Waters; but she appeared not to see him at all.

Waters cursed as his trusty vehicle rose to new heights and wafted him across the river altogether. This was the test, he reminded himself grimly. Would he live publicly or privately? Would one Bunny girl be enough to bring him down? No, he said to himself again and again as he strained through the binoculars at the receding scene. On no account. Never, no.

It was with some guilt that Waters realized he was going over the multi-level city and was too preoccupied to see it. Glancing backwards once, he thought he saw two black-robed figures toiling amongst the other workers at the top of a glittering skyscraper—and a small, bald man trying to pin a board on to the side of the rapidly rising building. B-O-W-L, Waters spelt out as he was blown violently to the south. Then his eyes began to sting from the wind, and he hid them behind calloused fingers.

But Waters knew he must land at the first sighting of open countryside. It was time now to think seriously of his mission—and to go back to the city if necessary to preach public living to the masses. First, a deep breath of pure downland air, a stretching of the arms and legs on grass nibbled by generations of sheep, a glimpse perhaps of the awesome stones of the Druids, whose mysteries he had fathomed on his lonely vigil in Hyde Park. What a contrast it would be to the dusty ruins of London! What freedom would be his as he strode, sole master of the breasts and vales and wooded plains of Southern England! His eyes wept in nostalgia despite himself.

From the great height of the balloon the land beneath looked strangely chalky—and dotted with black, like an over-enlarged photograph. No green anywhere; no trees, no lush meadows sprouting a second crop of buttercups. No white spots, their movements so mysterious to a possible visitor from outer space, running lethargically on a worn cricket pitch. No ponds, tadpole-shaped fragments of ancient glass, with their ducks and bodies of drowned witches in their silted depths. No horses, cows—no patchwork of fields, the mustard crop as bright as an iodined thumb. No thatched roofs, roses climbing over rat-infested rafters

In short, no countryside. The wind seemed to grow

tired at the realization that, blow as it might, no leaves would rustle, no branches would bend, no lakes would ruffle like the underfeathers of a bird—and it dropped, leaving Waters sinking low over the unrecognizable landscape.

He had no idea where he was now. Below, the white dormitory towns stretched as far as the eye could see: a silent, vast necropolis intersected by grey ribbons on which cars crawled like beetles along the legs and arms of the dead. Behind him towered the great complex structures of the city, swaying antennae precariously attached to an inert body. Clouds covered the sun, the air became heavy and humid. Waters felt a terrible, all-embracing fear.

He understood what he was seeing. The knowledge was too much for him to bear, and he threw out ballast wildly in a last effort to rise above it, to glide away across the sea to safety. The balloon rose a few feet, then dropped again. Waters closed his eyes in prayer. He forgot the new religion he had constructed with such care in his days as a hermit by the ruined shell of the Albert Hall. He forgot his mission to save the world. He wanted only one thing now—to survive.

When he opened his eyes, he found his worst suspicions confirmed.

What lay beneath him was—a termitary! Workers swarmed endlessly, tirelessly over the network of towers and passageways and cells-within-cells of the monstrous immobile organism.

Soldiers with tiny red guns guarded the inner and outer ramparts of the structure.

The digestive organs of the community lay directly

under him now. Canteens five miles long and ten miles wide gave off a shrill clatter of spoons on plates. Cities of latrines spread out beyond, the walls gaily painted to resemble English summer gardens. Pleasure palaces sported replicas of Palladian villas on their hanging terraces; on simulated motorways petrol-run cars crashed and burned, the flames extinguished instantly by horse-drawn fire-engines.

Waters's balloon drifted listlessly towards a great heap, as jumbled with bright stones and minarets as an Oriental temple. But as he approached he felt his pulse race, his heart beat noisily against his ribs. Something was drawing him down, down—

A light, green and luminous, streamed from the impossible building.

He saw a woman strolling in the labyrinth of courtyards beneath him. Her hair hung down her back like a sparkling fleece. A swarm of workers surrounded her, carrying fruit and mirrors in gold frames.

Waters prayed to be allowed to reach the ground. To serve her, to die in obedience for her was all he asked now. The Queen Ant, the brain of the brilliant mechanism!

The balloon sank lower and lower. The Queen looked up once and her eyes seemed to burn through Waters. The basket bumped once on to the ground—

A rush of air sounded through the stone-studded passages of the palace and ran through the lapidary maze like galloping horses. The Queen's hair blew out behind her in a shield of blinding light. The wind grew, lifting Waters's balloon like a toy and blowing it skywards, south, higher and higher until the termitary was no more than a piece of porous rock that lay half broken off from the mainland.

For Waters, trembling with gratitude at his freedom, could see from his great height both north and south of the Thames as he scudded across the angry skies.

Slowly the South of England was sinking into the sea. The Crack had severed it—and it broke off like the rim of a badly mended plate.

The wind roared and howled. Waters shivered in the icy cold. Miles below, like dwarf Japanese gardens, the tropical zones of Devon and Cornwall disappeared under the sea. Hotels and Hydrangeas formed sunken cities. Along the submerged golf courses fish swam lazily.

Waters's homeland disappeared from sight. Bravely, wrapping himself in his wife's anorak against the cold, he faced the future.